TECHSIKA

A JOURNEY

NEELAM JHA

Powered by

24by7Publishing.com

MRP: INR 349.00

First Published in October, 2023
Version 1.00
Printed in India
ISBN: 978-81-965785-1-0

Cover Design by 24by7 Publishing

Printing & Distribution of the book is powered by

24by7 Publishing
13 New Road, Kolkata - 51, India
https://www.24by7publishing.com
mail@24by7publishing.com
+91 9831 470 133
+91 9433 444 334

Powered by

24by7Publishing.com

To my father, Chandra Narayan Jha

&

my mother, Sita Jha

Bhagavad Gita says,

"A day without blessings of parents is the day without happiness and joy."

NOTE TO THE READER

Do the heroes possess supernatural powers to resolve crises at the click of a finger? Well, not always. My heroes in this story are neither larger-than-life characters nor legendary figures. They are part of the crowd just like you and me, and if the hour of reckoning approaches, they rise in the face of adversities. Of course, in today's digital world, instead of clicking a finger, they believe in clicking the mouse.

When I took voluntary retirement from a fruitful career with the Central Bank of India last year, I thought of celebrating the grit and determination of the common man and thus began the journey of TECHSIKA, the story of hope cast in the backdrop of a power tussle.

In this ongoing struggle, let me present to you the woman of substance - **Dr Chandrasi** (Chief Scientist, National Oceanic Defence Organisation), Niskashi's rebel prince - **Kamtej** (reputed Lawyer) and an idealist **Kraman** (Journalist) fighting the battle of Satya (*Truth*) vs Mithya (*Illusion*). It is not only their journey but ours, too, as the quest for TECHSIKA unfolds.

Part I of the story takes off on 12th March this year with flight UV 432 to Nabinagar, as National Oceanic Defence Organization is hit by a Ransomware attack. The second part zooms back to the eighties and nineties, culminating in December 2004, when the seeds of this saga were sown. Part III is set in the current times when all knives are out as we move towards a riveting climax near Tarulia. Can silence be golden when there is a concerted attack on Mother Nature?

Think and decide…

Acknowledgements

This book would not have been possible without the encouragement of my husband Ashok & my son Aman, who patiently went through the rough drafts and provided critical feedback. Right from the ideation phase to its completion, they were always there for me. Thank you for your bedrock support and unwavering belief in me as we crisscrossed India and Europe during the writing of this book. The blessings of my father-in-law, Tej Narayan Jha and mother-in-law, Kamla Devi, have been inspirational in the culmination of this book.

Prologue

Festival time @Panch Mukhi

Purno Sindhu festival was in full swing, and the traditional drum beats were resonating in the prevalent festive spirit of the five isles of Panch Mukhi. Far from the hustle and bustle of city life, the serene surroundings looked like a paradise immersed in equanimity. Numerous bioluminescent fishes blinking in the night sea appeared like classical floral motifs dancing gracefully in flowing patterns.

The vast blue expanse of water was glistening in the moonlight. Casting a blue hue to the isles, the panorama was nothing short of a soothing experience for the senses and sheer magic for the soul. The shining red-green hot tentacled algae swimming upwards on full moon night formed the background of this picturesque setting, adding to the sparkle and elegance of Panch Mukhi.

It all began in the morning with the blowing of conches and trumpets along with Surya Namaskar to pay obeisance to Mother Nature. The rising sun slowly covered the islands in its warmth as the local songs added to the symphony of playful waves. The shubh muhurat[1] was declared by Padhua

---

[1] *auspicious time*

Kaka for the evening puja. He was a walking encyclopaedia, well-versed in Vedas and Upanishads, and widely revered amongst the local population. Padhua Kaka meant Panditji in the Kharki language, and his deep knowledge of ancient rituals and holy texts had this title bestowed upon him.

It was also a day of village feast, and the tantalising aroma of freshly prepared delicacies filled the air. The five isle sisters seemed to hold hands in a pristine trance-like beauty surrounded by water. They were glistening like a dazzling flower on a full moon night amidst the hypnotic murmuring of the waves. Panch Mukhi looked like a show stopper, thus thought the Coast Guards who were patrolling that fateful night…

Almost an hour later, the waves got bigger with the echo of raspy rumblings. The smacking waves seemed to pummel the islands as if warning them of a sinister plot ahead. The erstwhile beautiful surroundings were now appearing anxious and ominous. In the star-lit night of Purno Sindhu, the fireworks were getting bigger, perhaps signalling that there would be no more nights of festivities. Was it a brewing storm or the curse of the powerful Samudro Vritra[2]?

The youngsters of nearby Tarulia village had heard many stories of the rituals at the Purno Sindhu festival at Panch Mukhi from Padhua Kaka. But none of them seemed real tonight. The villagers who had assembled on the shore to watch the firecrackers were terrified as the deadly waves turned fiercer. They wanted to shout and swim to the aid of Padhua Kaka and all those at Panch Mukhi, but their limbs

---

[2] *Ocean Demon*

seemingly slumped, and their voices got numbed by the petrifying visuals.

The local boatmen from neighbouring areas had gathered on the shore, but the deafening sounds of explosions pushed them back. They all kept praying to Samudra Dev[3] to protect Padhua Kaka and all others at Panch Mukhi. But their voices and hope grew fainter as the night progressed.

By the time the Coast Guard's medical unit arrived, no sign of human life was visible. The Panch Mukhi flower, the pride of Varidhi[4], had disappeared. The ocean looked calm again, showing no remorse whatsoever. All that it left behind was an eerie silence and a smell of devastation pervading the air. What happened to the families that night? How would one know?

Although villagers of Tarulia were spared from the wrath of the Samudra Vritra on that fateful night, the unbearable anguish of not being able to rescue their friends turned into a personal trauma for each one of them. They were scarred for life. Were their emotional wounds ever going to heal?

A few hours later, an undersea earthquake with a magnitude of 9.1 triggered the Tsunami of December 2004, killing thousands of people across a dozen countries.

---

[3] *Ocean God*

[4] *Ocean*

Part I

Fasten your seat belts,
Turbulence ahead…

I

Vistaar hai apaar, praja dono paar kare hahakaar, nishabd sada O' Ganga tum, Ganga bahti ho kyun? [5]

The bard of Brahmaputra's melodious voice filled Kraman with nostalgia. He stood on the balcony of his sixth-floor flat, mesmerised by the maestro's emotional, poetic composition and traditional folk music. Newly blossomed flowers in the earthy terracotta pots also seemed to be dancing merrily to the tunes as the newspaper landed near his left foot with a slight sound. He looked down and waved to the paper delivery boy, who was now aiming at another flat. Such a throw and so much precision; it was admirable!

He picked up the newspaper, and the first page was filled with exit poll results of the Vidhan Sabha elections 2023 being held in three states. Most of the pollsters' predictions were in favour of JSP (Jan Sampark Party) coming to power. The counting day was just seventy-two hours away.

JSP, founded in 1994 by Mamak Vragji, was eyeing a major role at the national level. The relatively young party in electoral politics had traits of a marathon runner showing no signs of fatigue. A win in all three states would make them the main opposition to the incumbent ruling party at the Centre. Their clout in the Upper House would rise, too.

---

[5] *People who live along expansive stretches on your sides are in turmoil, O Ganga! Why do you always flow quietly?*

The fate of the political parties had been sealed in the EVM[6]s. But 'there are many slips between the cup and lip'. On the fifteenth of March, it would come to light whether the exit polls were right about the people's mandate.

Kraman shared his birthday with Jan Sampark Party's foundation day in March, and his friends often poked fun at him for the celebrations being held all across the country coinciding with his birthday.

It was a bright, sunny Sunday and a holiday after two weeks. Being a part of the media fraternity had its benefits, but it also entailed long working hours with fewer holidays. "Maybe 'Jage Raho' (*stay awake*) should be our new tagline," chuckled Kraman.

"No work today," Kraman said to himself as he booked tickets for the DOTA (Defence of the Ancients) tournament at the State E-sports championship. The game would have continued in his thoughts had it not been for the sound of the doorbell.

As he reluctantly opened the door, there was no one outside. "Maybe some kid or prankster," he thought. But wait; there was an envelope near the doormat. He once again looked in the corridor for the visitor who had dropped the envelope but drew a blank.

He picked up the hand-painted envelope. It looked somewhat familiar. The same sun-dried colours and a similar pattern of large Kadamba trees near the Krishna temple. "No, it can't be

---

[6] *Electronic Voting Machine*

true," thought Kraman as he trembled and the envelope slipped from his hands. He lifted himself from the floor and gulped a glass of water. The envelope looked old but seemingly had been well-preserved by its holder. He picked it up and held it close to his heart and could instantly feel the warmth of Suchita didi. It had been so many years since he last saw her at Chandinagar.

His hands shook like a leaf as he opened the envelope. It contained to and fro flight tickets in his name to Nabinagar and a hotel booking voucher at Moksha, but wait; there was something else, too. It looked like white glistening sand but seemed denser than it. The name Nabinagar rang a bell in his mind. He had seen it somewhere recently.

Oh yes! The annual Dinkar journalism awards ceremony at Nand Gaon, when a twisted paper had fallen from his colleague Shlok's pocket while he was taking out the mobile. Kraman picked up the paper and waved at him, but he exited in a hurry.

"Was it a rough paper?" Thought Kraman as he spread it on his palm? It was a small hand-sketched map. There was a dense forest near the ocean… what was the name? Kraman tried to recall. Aha, it was Sona Ghaati, and then there was a road leading to Nabinagar Airport. In the midst of this map was written TECHSIKA in bold letters with a question mark.

The next morning, when he looked for Shlok in the office,he came to know that Shlok had resigned due to personal reasons. He spoke to his Editor about the incident, who suggested that the paper be handed over to Harmeet, who was now looking after the responsibilities of Shlok. Kraman did not pursue the matter further, and now, a month later, a ticket to Nabinagar propped right at his doorstep.

He closed the envelope neatly and put it in his bag. Kraman was in two minds as he looked at the flight tickets again. "Oh, the tickets are for today itself. It looks like some kind of emergency situation! Is there a story waiting at Nabinagar? I need to check. I can't afford to miss the bus, rather the flight in this case."

He tried calling Shlok's number, but the incoming call facility had been barred on it. There was not much time, so he emailed the latest developments to his editor.

All the time, he could not take his eyes away from the envelope, which had the beautiful signature of Suchita didi artistically hidden in the design. His fingers held the envelope, the same way he held her hands on the first day of school.

"I need to pack up fast; there is not much time left. It would be better to keep my passport and visa also, in case I don't get time to repack my things or if my stay at Nabinagar gets extended."

That reminded him of twenty-first March when he was accompanying the media team to cover the esteemed Ocean Research Organization's annual event in Vienna.

Packing was almost done; he kept his laptop, charger and power bank in the backpack. On the way to the Airport , he rechecked the envelope, phone and his passport. Looking at the passport, he was reminded of the delay in getting his visa due to the passport having his name as Kraman Kraman (repeating the first name as he did not carry a surname).

Actually, his parents had decided against the use of the family surname in his name. They believed in the One Nation Theory, where all citizens were equals and nationality was their prime identity. Perhaps they were unaware of the importance of surnames, particularly in passports and visas by many countries. In spite of various biometric identifications available even in this digital age, this surname criterion had often caused delays for him at visa and immigration counters.

As the taxi stopped at the red traffic light, he could see his favourite Japanese restaurant, 'Oishii', on the left side of the road. "Being Sunday, it would open at 2 p.m.," said Kraman aloud. The delectable Sushi menu and his favourite 'Samurai Maki' would have continued in his thoughts had his phone not vibrated. It was a message from an unknown number – 'Use India's Independence Day in dd-mm-yyyy format to open your gift at the Moksha Hotel. Happy Journey, Kraman, and see you at Nabinagar.'

He was surprised by the sponsor's gesture of booking the executive suite at five-star Moksha hotels for him. It felt like some sort of VIP treatment. What a silly thought, he corrected himself.

"I seem to be rating myself too high. After all, I am just a young journalist trying to create awareness about conservation of marine biodiversity through my articles in newspapers. For some, it may sound like a bit of scientific gibberish and as far as the scientific community is concerned, I am a learner who still has a long way to go."

But then, working for one of the biggest media houses in the country was no mean achievement, and it did add weight to his name and maybe represented power in the eyes of some people! "Power, the most powerful word in the dictionary,is like dynamite. When used responsibly, millions are benefitted. But what if it falls in the hands of wrong people?"

A few hours later, he was onboard flight UV 432, supercharged with the hope that the sender of the envelope would affirm Suchita didi's wellbeing. The flight seemed far from busy. With seventy-odd passengers on board, there was room for everyone to spread out their legs and take a nap. But his mind was preoccupied with the envelope, and his heart seemed to be racing faster than the taxiing plane. Was Suchita didi connected with the sender of the envelope? The questions were aplenty, and answers scarce.

His thoughts were interrupted by the sudden rumblings and commotion in the plane. There seemed to be some sort of turbulence with a lot of screaming sounds. Was it due to bad weather? As he opened his eyes, Kraman could see two men with guns. They had covered their faces with masks, so not much was visible. But both had a tall, athletic build with a gruff voice. One of them pointed a gun at the cabin crew and threatened to blow up the plane. It is a hijack, yelled his partner. All of you put your heads down, he ordered menacingly. Kraman looked at his watch; the flight had covered almost two-thirds of the journey.

The pilot was left with no option but to reluctantly open the door for the second hijacker. As the cockpit door closed, a burly passenger seized the opportunity and flung himself on the lone hijacker standing near him. Emboldened by his move, two more passengers stood up and moved swiftly towards the hijacker.

Then, a gunshot rang, and the first passenger was down. His arm was bleeding profusely. Although the shot seemed accidental, it sent shivers down the spine. It was a grim reminder that the lives of all the passengers were at stake. That single shot seemed to immobilise the rest of the passengers, and all put their heads down as instructed by the hijacker.

The hijacker was now moving towards the business class. As the separating curtain between business and economy classes had been pulled off by the hijackers, Kraman could see that there was only a single person on the aisle seat of the front row. The hijacker pulled her hand, forcing her to stand up. But why had he picked her out of so many passengers?

From his fifth-row aisle seat, Kraman could see a saree-clad, bespectacled, tall woman, possibly in her late fifties, with slightly grey hair neatly plaited into a tight bun, resisting the attempted removal of her eyeglasses. As she turned back during the scuffle, her face became visible to all the passengers. Oh my god, she is Dr Chandrasi, the internationally renowned marine biologist and Chief Scientist of the National Oceanic Defence Organisation (NODO)! But what is she doing here?

"Is she the target? Or does she have something important in her possession? But how do they intend to take her out from an airborne aircraft? Are they planning to divert the flight and land at some other Airport?" Kraman's journalistic instinct was searching for motives.

The hijacker was looking at his watch time and again. "Was he waiting for someone or something? It seems like a time-bound operation," thought Kraman as he continued watching the hijacker from the corner of his eye, trying to anticipate their next move.

Kraman was also trying to look for the sky marshal in the flight. Since they were deployed on a random basis, he was not sure if there was one among the passengers. "That means Dr Chandrasi is on an unofficial visit," thought Kraman. Otherwise, her security or at least the sky marshal, would have been on board.

He was busily deciphering the reasons for Dr Chandrasi's zero security travel arrangement when he saw the first hijacker forcing something on her face. It looked like some sort of iris verification device. But he couldn't be sure from a distance as it was a small device.

She started coughing and fell to the ground. Her body lay motionless as the hijacker kicked her legs. When she didn't get up, he panicked and bent down to lift her up and then what happened next was unimaginable.

There was a loud scream as Dr Chandrasi's left palm struck a blow at the hijacker's chest. He fell to the ground, writhing in pain. Like an experienced Kalari practitioner, she silenced her opponent in a single blow. A classic example of hitting a vital point in the body known as the marmam. Kraman was mesmerised by such a precise combination of techniques of Kalaripayattu[7].

He had seen these techniques in his favourite online game, 'Prey - Hunter or Hunted', but all those moves looked naïve

---

[7] *famous Martial Art form of Kerala*

today in comparison to this live performance. The game, in spite of all its visual effects, did not stand a chance against her killer moves. Here she was, the lone warrior in a Marathi nauvari style saree, hunting the hunter. One thing was certain; her Kalaripayattu moves were just like a Gurukkal with the meticulous combination of Chuvadu and Vadivu (i.e. steps & postures, respectively).

At that point, the second hijacker opened the cockpit door. But before he could move, she sprang on him like a tigress and pinned him down with her knee. Then, using her left arm, she stuck his forehead like lightning. Her alacrity and swiftness took the hijacker by surprise. 'Meyy kanavanam', as they say, meaning making the body an eye, she proved that the hijackers were no match to her experience and skills.

Then she took out a device from her hand luggage kept in the upper compartment, which looked like some kind of body scanner from a distance to Kraman. She was seemingly checking the hijackers for any firearms or bombs on them. As the device emitted a green light, she asked the flight attendants to tie the unconscious hijackers tightly to the front row seat.

Meanwhile, pilots were in communication with the ATC (Air Traffic Control), and soon, the plane made an emergency landing at Nabinagar Airport amidst a lot of confusion and chaos on the ground as well as inside the plane. Ambulances, doctors, firefighters, and security people were all waiting on the tarmac. The passengers clapped continuously and cheered Dr Chandrasi as the Pilot announced, "Passengers to remain seated till the seat belt signs are on."

Soon, the gates of the aircraft opened, and commandos rushed in from the front door and escorted Dr Chandrasi to safety. There was a car waiting for her on the tarmac itself, which sped away immediately. The two hijackers were then taken away on stretchers along with the injured passenger.

Once again, the security personnel entered the aircraft with a bag. They asked all of us to put our phones, electronics and other digital devices in the bag and requested to keep our boarding passes in hand. Not more than five minutes had elapsed since the landing, but the wait appeared so long. All of us were dying to touch the ground at Nabinagar Airport.

It was the Pilot again, "Passengers to exit from the rear door of the aircraft," and this time, his voice sounded like music to the ears. We were led down a darkened corridor to a hall for medical examination by the team of doctors. Special care was being taken of the injured passenger, who seemed to be responding well to the treatment. Many of the passengers were crying and hugging each other, as some were thanking God for saving their lives.

But there was one passenger whose behaviour as well as dress sense seemed awkward, to say the least. Kraman nicknamed him Lal Kaka[8] due to his bizarre sense of dressing in red colour. He was wearing a bright red suit with a big red hat. His face did not look normal; it appeared as if he was wearing prosthetics. Even from a long distance, this man was easily visible due to his oversized sunglasses. Kraman was puzzled to see his calmness in such an explosive situation.

---

[8] *red uncle*

Lal Kaka had absolutely no reaction, as if he was oblivious to his surroundings or else he was damn sure of everything around him. His Parkinsonian gait was peculiar, to say the least. It was such a copybook motion that it was difficult to say whether he was acting or not?

The whole process, including the critical incident debriefing, took more than four hours before being cleared by the security team, and thereafter, Kraman received his mobile and laptop. He mentioned the Moksha Hotel as his place of stay, and then something caught his eye. Lal Kaka, who signed in the register just ahead of him as Lal Kunwar, had also mentioned the same hotel as his destination!

The car sent by the hotel was waiting for him in the parking area of the Airport. Soon, Kraman was racing towards Hotel Moksha. He closed his eyes and tried to reconstruct the hijack drama as it had unfolded in front of his eyes a few hours earlier. There seemed to be something unusual about it. The hijackers never made any demand.

Was it a case of a plan gone awry or a design to cover something more sinister? The car screeched to a halt. "Have we reached?" Kraman asked, rolling down his glass window, but it was pitch dark outside.

"No sir, I had to apply sudden brakes as one cyclist was crossing the road", said his driver. Actually, the Panch Mukhi memorial is just on the other side of the road. Lots of people come to pray here for their near and dear ones whom they lost on that ill-fated night in 2004. Even after so many years, the stinging pain in our hearts refuses to go, the driver said in a misty voice.

"Yes, it was very tragic," said Kraman as he asked the driver to stop for a moment so that he could pay his respects at the memorial.

"We will reach in five to ten minutes, sir," said the driver as Kraman came back. "Actually, the Airport is situated on the western outskirts of the town, and your hotel is almost on the other side, near the ocean. The hotel rooms have an excellent view. It is nice that you have arrived here at night and have been spared the daytime traffic snarls."

As the car reached the driveway of the hotel, Kraman thanked his driver and immediately took the keys from the reception. His room was on the top floor with a glass ceiling just over the bed. Completely exhausted by the day's events, he jumped onto the soft king-size bed to get some rest. Tomorrow was the big day as his mysterious sponsor was expected to show up.

At about 5 a.m., his phone started ringing. Who could it be at this time? Kraman silenced the ringer and put his head beneath the pillow in a bid to get some more sleep. The phone rang again. He picked it up this time, sensing the caller's urgency. It was his team lead, but so early in the morning? She was speaking in a high-pitched voice, and her tone indicated that it was something very important. However, due to disturbances in the line, her voice was not clear, and suddenly the phone got disconnected. "Perhaps network issues," thought Kraman as her message beeped on his phone.

"Kavya is dead."

II

Kamtej, the famous Lawyer, was on his way to the rally at Fauz Maidan, near Rainbow Conclave. Normally, he would charge a princely amount per hearing, but today, he had come of his own free will to Sona Ghaati (Golden Valley), a remote place for the urban intelligentsia. How could he refuse Sarpanch's[9] request for an issue that was so close to his own heart?

He renounced the crown many years ago, as the weight of heirdom on his conscience had become too much to bear. He could no longer be on the same page as his father, Maharaja Shakti Shubhankar (the erstwhile owner of these lands), who wallowed in his sense of entitlement and social status and lacked the courage of conviction to stand up for what is right.

It was an hour's drive to the venue, but today the roads were full. The villagers had assembled all along the rickety village roads to have a glimpse of their messiah. Slogans like 'Nature is our mother', 'Save Nature for a better future', and 'Maa aur maati se bane Sona Ghaati' (*Sona Ghaati is our mother and motherland*) reverberated with the drum beats all the way.

In the era of omnipresent social media where the net is meant to catch eyeballs rather than fish, the shelf life of news is on the wane, lamented the Sarpanch."My son is always surfing

---

[9] *village head*

the net, some new video keeps coming up and he remains hooked. He is more interested in cosmetic changes in the system, maybe because it takes lesser time."

Kamtej nodded as he recalled last night's discussion on "Future versus Nature" on a popular channel wherein the articulate anchor was citing various global growth models. Whether merely waxing eloquently about growth strategies made any difference at ground level, Kamtej was not sure!

He wished that these affected villagers had also been called for that discussion. Perhaps the difference between reel and real would have made the discourse more impactful for the viewers! These villagers had not heard terms like El Nino or La Nina, but weren't they the ones whose survival was at stake, Kamtej thought for a while. Or maybe the air-conditioned speakers were in denialist mode, wantonly cold-shouldering the stark truth.

The lives as well as livelihoods of these villagers had been dependent on nature for ages. Being at the lowest rung of the food supply chain, they bore the brunt of environmental devastation and were many times ignored by the people drunk on power.

Over the years, the traditional synergy between human beings and nature has weakened due to the greed of a section of people bent upon exploiting nature without considering the needs of our future generations. The age-old coexistence model was seemingly being sacrificed on the altar of unidirectional expansive growth."With just nine days to go for the international day of forests, weren't such tragic incidents a travesty?"

Tears brimmed in Kamtej's eyes as he looked at the kisan[10] raising slogans on the roads. Perhaps they were angry due to their voices being silenced by the power lobbies and felt that they had been side-lined with little or no say in policies being made for them. How could Kamtej turn a blind eye to this sheer nescience by the authorities?

For generations, farming had been their primary source of income at Sona Ghaati. Now, suddenly, everything was being taken away from them for the sake of an upcoming fancy resort. The indigenous natives were being asked to make way for the tourists in the resort so that they could showcase the rich heritage of Sona Ghaati. Wasn't it a calculated design of the socio-political elites to sacrifice the sustainable development model? These people were to be relocated to Rainbow City. But bereft of joys and colours in their lives, how could they form a rainbow or even be a part of it?

And all this in the name of economic sensibility by mighty PENAK Associates and their suave CEO Atrin Kumar!!! 'Pen is mightier than sword' – was a well-suited tagline for the company. Actually, its name itself was a combination of PEN & AK (Atrin Kumar). In the last decade, the company had risen as a colossal monolith, gobbling up all the competition that came its way.

The brilliant, consummate networking giant Atrin Kumar had become the undisputable czar of industry. With shareholders lapping up generous dividends and the loyalist directors endorsing all his decisions, there was nothing that could stop him. Buyouts, takeovers, acquisitions, and mergers, he used

---

[10] *farmer*

every style in the book to create and consolidate his footprints in the country.

The modus operandi was simple: first, he captured the market using predatory pricing, and as the company gained monopoly, the pricing patterns were accordingly changed to its advantage. PENAK Associates enjoyed unparalleled brand value & customer trust. It had an indelible presence in the market, courtesy of Atrin's Midas touch. He was at the right place and at the right time, always in the good books of the powers that be.

Atrin was shrewd enough to keep his personal choices at arm's length so that they did not cloud his professional decisions. Being a level-headed guy, he was aware of the pitfalls of inroads made by outsiders in business, be it Godmen or politicians. He steered clear of both, but politician Mamak Vragji was an exception. He was a dear friend.

But can there be smoke without fire? The media reports here and there about the mining leases and not-so-eco-friendly tactics of PENAK Associates used to crop up from time to time. The questions regarding opacity, lack of disclosures, inflated valuations, and debt-laden balance sheets at PENAK Associates were also red-flagged on a few occasions, calling for intense scrutiny.

But no investigation was available on record. 'Paisa bolta hai' (*money talks/exerts influence*), perhaps the power of money suppressed the brewing storms. The complainants often disappeared within hours of the alleged complaints.

The recent induction of Kavya as a majority stakeholder in PENAK Associates did raise a few eyebrows. The outlandish decision would have fizzled out had the scandalous rumours not surfaced about Kavya seeking a paternity test against the real estate baron Shyam Pradosh.

It was not that anybody doubted her leadership abilities, but the interest in her legal battle had a bigger audience, and the media trial was already blaring on social networking sites. Panel discussions were telecast as courtroom proceedings, with anchors keen on delivering their opinions as the verdict. Naturally, people grew curious to know whether Shyam Pradosh was, in fact, Kavya's biological father.

Kavya, the latest unicorn in the business world, was a successful entrepreneur who did everything in style. The media seemed to be head over heels for following her. It was not their fault. Anyone who met her once would vouch for her distinctive personality. She had a special kind of straightforwardness which would make people around her see reason instantaneously. And the best part was, she felt neither afraid to address the elephant in the room nor made any pretences about its presence.

He met Kavya six months ago at the City fundraiser gala, where he was asked to fill in for the regular reporter. Many times, the limelight of such events is more on the celebrities rather than the cause, said one of his friends at the media house. So Kraman went there expecting it to be a formal event with speeches and normal thanksgiving stuff.

The organisers of the event wanted great coverage, and hence, a big contingent of media fraternity had descended at the venue. They were just five minutes into the programme when the commotion began. The cameras turned away from the main stage and focused on the entry gate.

Kavya's infectious smile literally lit up the hall. Her sparkling eyes spoke of a beautiful soul reminiscent of a fire crackling against the ice. Wearing a Prada Sable Jacquard jumpsuit with her signature Versace scarf, she walked in with grace and poise.

She declined the invitation to join the celebrities on the dais and moved towards the end of the hall where the homeless orphan kids were sitting. By now, Kraman was sure of one thing: she had a magnetic personality, and the cameras followed her instantaneously. Unmindful of the surroundings, she shook hands with the kids and patted their backs.

Then, holding hands, they all moved towards the dais. The dais would not accommodate the celebrities and the kids together, the anchor protested feebly. But she was used to having her way and continued to march towards the dais. Sensing her defiance, the anchor requested the celebrities to move towards the main area. Soon, Kavya and the kids were sitting on the stage under the arch lights. The self-effacing, gracious diva thought for a while and then handed over the mike to the kids. They were initially hesitant, but soon, they opened up about their lives, struggles and the discrimination being faced by them.

Kraman and many others in the audience were virtually crying at their plight, hoping that a day would come soon when our children don't have to confront such inhuman conditions!

Many of them aspired to be teachers, policemen, doctors, etc. With moist eyes, she asked if they wished to perform on the stage. The kids looked at each other for a few moments, and then one of them started singing Gandhiji's favourite bhajan, and soon all of them joined in. The kids' loud voices singing - "Raghupati Raghav Raja Ram, Patit Pawan Sita Ram" soon filled the entire room as the audience, too, chipped in.

She took out an envelope from her bag and gave it to the anchor before bidding goodbye to the kids. In a choked voice, she said thank you as she handed over the mike back to the anchor and exited the venue unannounced, just as she had entered.

The programme continued, but Kraman had lost interest. He was now curious to know about the envelope which she had given to the anchor. There was a lot of clapping going on as the celebrities began pledging their contributions to the cause. Towards the end of the programme, the anchor came on the stage and drew out the envelope that Kavya had given him. Madam had specifically instructed the envelope be opened towards the end of the programme, said the anchor.

As the anchor opened the envelope and started reading, the expression on his face changed from bewilderment to disbelief. She had donated 'Rameshwaram', her seaside villa, to these kids and had created a fund of Rs. five million as an initial corpus for funding their education. Her Trust was going to take care of all the needs of these kids from here on.

Today's function has changed so many lives. Now, these children had a home called Rameshwaram and an angel guardian named Kavya. Most importantly, they now had a family to call their own. There was a stunning silence in the hall, followed by a deafening clapping sound.

As expected, the next-day newspapers had articles appreciating her munificence and the sound bite given to one of the leading channels. "I believe in generosity rather than charity" went viral on social media. Kraman had heard this phrase earlier also, but coming from her, it didn't sound cliché. Actually, it sounded like a heartfelt, genuine feeling of a compassionate individual.

Other contributors to the charity event, too, had been pretty generous to the cause. However, her style of delivery ensured that the issues pertaining to homeless orphan kids got the coverage and attention they deserved.

How could she go away so soon? His heart was aching at the loss of a great human being. Social media was abuzz with conspiracy angles and suicide theories. Motives like revenge were also doing the rounds. Comforting the afflicted and afflicting the comfortable was her way of life. Had she crossed paths with the comfortable folks and paid the price?

III

Dr Chandrasi was on her way back from the Nabinagar Airport when she received news about the ransomware attack at NODO (National Oceanic Defence Organisation). The very first thought that flashed in her mind, was the attack intentionally planned at a time when she was airborne and physically inaccessible to her team? But very few people were privy to her travel plans to Nabinagar. Then how did this information leak out?

She was expecting the truth to be unearthed soon as the hijackers were in the custody of NIU (National Intelligence Unit). Her car was swiftly racing towards the satellite office of NODO at Nabinagar, as her mind was grappling with various probabilities. The hijack and ransomware attack at the same time could not be washed off as a mere coincidence.

The second shift staff members were settling in their seats at NODO when the Orange alert was sounded. 'Emergency alert, all hands on deck' beeped on their internal phones. "It must be a drill," said a staff member. "Oh no, the systems have begun to shut down," said another. 'The systems will be inaccessible for the next three minutes,' it was Security Chief Chaya's voice. The quad group rushed towards the Lambda Con, where Dr Chandrasi and Chaya were waiting for them.

"No time for pleasantries, guys," said Dr Chandrasi, as one of the members rose to wish her 'Good Afternoon'. And then she dropped the bombshell. "There has been a LockBit ransomware attack on our systems this morning." The quad's facial expression turned from disbelief to denial, and none of them spoke a single word. There was stunned silence for a few seconds, followed by murmurs. "Ransomware attacks could disable our operations and have a profound impact on TECHSIKA. Did they ask for ransom?" One member raised his hand.

"Yes, they asked for passcodes. But don't worry, the incident has been contained by our cyber security team," said Dr Chandrasi in her reassuring tone, "The EDR (Endpoint Detection and Response) controls stopped the initial exploitation and subsequent spread." But she could see that the mention of passcodes caused a major flutter in the hall. Bewilderment was evident on everyone's face.

"But it is our top secret national programme; how did they have this information?" There were again murmurs in the hall. Do the attackers also have information about AMBAK-the EYE?

Dr Chandrasi looked at her team and said, "It's their uncanny style of venturing into NODO, practically a lion's den, that worries me. Prahar[11] by stealth is a common strategy for enemy groups, but announcing one's entry in this way by sounding the gong in broad daylight is strange. Perhaps this is a new group that does not believe in standard warfare. Their confidence shows that they have an ace up their sleeves, and we are still in the dark about it."

---

[11] *attack*

The only fact that forced an assuring smile on Dr Chandrasi's face was that the enemy was not aware of their third layer of security. Passcodes and iris authentication were the two primary layers which had been attacked today. But none of them would have worked without the third one. It was the most important layer, known only to a select group of people.

Chaya's team briefed all the members about the incident in its entirety as per standard operating protocol. The members sitting in the observation centre were keenly waiting for the servers to restart.

"NODO's infallibility and invincibility is the pride of its staff members, and the enemy hit them where it hurt the most. I must speak immediately to the National Investigation Unit Chief, De Silva Sir. This attempted breach could have serious repercussions on our project," she said, looking at the downcast faces of staff from the glass walls of Lambda Con.

"Ah! Dr Chandrasi, what a coincidence! I was just going to call you," Chief De Silva's voice was tense as he spoke about the presence of toxic MNG capsules in the hijacker's blood.

"MNG!" Dr Chandrasi was shell-shocked. "But how is that possible, Sir? This drug is not something one can procure over the counter."

"Well, my toxicology team confirmed the use of MNG," said the Chief solemnly, "and I think that clears the confusion about the plan of hijackers. They never had any intention of blowing up the plane or landing at some other Airport. I am not sure whether the hijackers knew that it was a suicide mission and the MNG had been given to them on purpose.

But both of them weighed exactly sixty kilograms and were given identical fatal doses of three milligrams per kilo of their body weight, just before they boarded the flight. The flight duration was of one hour and twenty-five minutes, and MNG takes two hours to dissolve in the blood. As you know, it kills by interfering with sodium ion channels in the cells of muscles and nerves, jamming them open so that they do not close. So, whichever way the hijack went, they were not supposed to live to see its outcome."

"Yes, MNG is fatal," said Dr Chandrasi in an alarmed tone.

"The continued migration of sodium ions immobilises the nervous system, and once it disintegrates fully, the person dies within seconds. And that is its important characteristic. Till one hundred nineteen minutes, the person shows very few symptoms, but in the last minute, he suddenly collapses. In those deadly sixty seconds, the blood supply is frozen, and the nerves begin to crack. Death is instant, with almost nil chances of survival."

"Now I understand why the hijackers were continuously looking at their watches," said Dr Chandrasi. "It was not a sign of their nervousness. They had been instructed to land the plane at its scheduled time, and hence, they asked the pilots to continue its original path with no diversions. So is it the end of the road?" asked Dr Chandrasi.

"Not at all! Here is the good news," De Silva remarked, "Our investigations have revealed that there was one more passenger in cahoots with the hijackers. The three of them were communicating on the walkie-talkie. We are looking for that third passenger. He is still on the loose, but we hope to capture him soon.

As the hijack failed, it appeared that he chose to mingle with the group of passengers to save himself. Perhaps he feared for his safety and, in his nervousness, left the walkie-talkie inside the plane. So yes, we have his fingerprints on it, but there are multiple prints.

Since it almost looked like a mini toy, someone put it in the baggage overhead compartment. My team was alerted when we found the other two devices in the hijacker's possession. As we are speaking, my team is matching it with our database. It might take some time.

My team has also retrieved the broken irisometer[12], and understandably, Chandrasi, you were their target. We are looking at various angles. Maybe the third partner on the plane was the kingpin, or maybe all three of them were mere foot soldiers? The investigations are underway; I will keep you in the loop if something new comes up."

"Thanks, Sir," said Dr Chandrasi before hanging up.

She bowed to her Appa's (father) portrait on the table. It was on his insistence that she joined the Kalaripayattu Gurukulam as a nine-year-old. Nobody would have imagined that her training would one day safeguard the secrets of motherland. Her Appa meant the world to her, and she proudly reiterated this on public platforms. Her Women's Day speech a couple of days ago also began with her favourite line: "Behind every successful woman is a man". Had he not been so supportive, it would have been very difficult for her to reach the pinnacle as an internationally acclaimed scientist.

---

[12] *a device used for the capture of live iris and generally used as an identifier*

She looked at the NODO's computers; they were up and running again and the staff members were back at their respective terminals.

The last few hours since she boarded the flight (UV 432), had been baffling, to say the least. In this live battle of wits today, she had managed to defend NODO. But her experience forewarned that infuriated by the failure of the hijack plan, a deadlier assault could be on the anvil tomorrow. Her team needed to be on high alert.

Dr Chandrasi and her team had been working relentlessly to delve into the wonders of the ocean, and it was their research that led to a new discovery of inactive hydrothermal vents and massive seafloor sulphide deposits. Mining of these vents without a proper study of geological and biological inventory could lead to the loss of organisms living there and adversely impact the biodiversity equilibrium.

But the mining mafia was hell-bent on disrupting marine biodiversity and destroying their habitats.

Dr Chandrasi could feel the ocean's seething anger at this ecological imbalance."The once tranquil expanse of the ocean is slowly turning into a dump yard where plastic debris and other toxic wastages are swirling like a tempest. The vibrancy of coral reefs is being taken away, turning them into bleached and barren surfaces. It is a wake-up call for humanity, a desperate plea for restoration, conservation and balance."

Biodiversity is the fruit of billions of years of evolution, shaped by natural processes. But the diversity within species and between species is declining faster than at any other time in human history. The impact of the loss of biodiversity will have to be borne by us. The price that we will be forced to pay for this destruction is unknown, but our fate as a species hangs in the balance. She closed her eyes and exhaled deeply. Then she spoke in an infuriated tone, "We seem to be forgetting that our future is deeply connected to the health of our oceans."

NODO's objective was to protect the vents from illegal miners and safeguard the ocean reserves."After all, the wealth of our oceans is not only for us but also for our future generations."

Dr Chandrasi was leading her team in devising eco-friendly techniques to extract the deep sea deposits without upsetting nature's equilibrium. Deep sea mining needs a range of enabling technologies, and NODO had got a breakthrough. The prototype 'Akshay' had cleared all quality control checks as a less invasive tool that avoided stirring sediment or crushing life on the ocean floor while collecting deep-sea minerals. It was designed to selectively pick up the nodules using smart machine vision. Akshay could make rapid decisions on the basis of what it saw in spite of haze, diffraction, scattering, and low illumination that is prevalent on the ocean bed.

But it was the making of AMBAK - the EYE that had created a storm in the international arena.NODO's Research & Development wing had developed it at about half the cost of competing international products. Laced with Artificial Intelligence and Machine Learning, the cutting edge fifth generation system could autonomously detect various types of underwater threats like divers, submarines and UAVs (Underwater Autonomous Vehicles) with precision.

Packed with a new-age electronic and software suite, it was designed to defend the deep ocean treasures without adversely affecting the natural aquatic ecosystem. AMBAK- the EYE's protection software suite (Kavach), used deep learning for enhanced threat identification. It was programmed to recognize underwater threats, including those attempting to mask their presence as some noisy civilian cargo ship or tourist yachts. The EYE could see everything!

Its passive nature, which ensured minimal impact on the surrounding aquatic life, was an added advantage. It stayed like deadwood on the ocean bed and sprang to life only when activated by NODO. And in case of attack, it had the ability to send a signal in less than thirty seconds. The response time taken by the advanced weapon unit, was under three minutes to wipe out the enemy, lock stock and barrel. It was meant to protect TECHSIKA, but what if the protector itself was under siege?

Today morning's double attack was a pointer to the fact that there was someone other than the core members of NODO who knew about the underwater secrets as well as the indigenous technologies at NODO, which could change this magic sand to ..

"The wolf in sheep's clothing needs to be identified urgently. The clock is ticking fast."

IV

Kamtej was a ray of hope, a beacon for the downtrodden and marginalised sections of society, whose voices were many a time muzzled by powerful people. His vehicle was stopped a few kilometres before the Fauz Maidan on the pretext of disturbance in law and order! There was a heavy police deployment with the posse of policemen guarding the area. He could see from the car that the surging groups of angry supporters were getting closer to the barricade.

Sensing the mood, Kamtej asked the Sarpanch to assist the police in maintaining law and order. Ask your supporters to follow the administrative orders; we are here to protest peacefully and not to create a ruckus, he told the Sarpanch as they stepped out of the car.

Sec 144 has been clamped in the area around Fauz Maidan till tomorrow morning, i.e. 13th of March. These people cannot go with you, the police officer on duty told Kamtej. No vehicle will be allowed to pass the barricades, he added sternly. Looking at his watch, Kamtej thought that there was enough time for him to reach the rally. He called the Sarpanch and discussed the situation with him.

Instead of accompanying him in the protest march, it was decided that the villagers would sit on a dharna[13] till sunset at

---

[13] *sit-in*

Sona Ghaati. He addressed the crowd briefly and requested them to follow the police orders. "Those sitting on the fences in the conflict between powerful and powerless people, cannot be called neutral. They are doing a disservice to humanity. Their indifference means that they are actually siding with the powerful people, adding to their might" , he said exhorting the people to stand together in this fight and join hands in 'Save Sona Ghaati Campaign'.

Then, in true Gandhian style, he decided to walk alone to Fauz Maidan. It was literally a walk down the memory lane, as part of Sona Ghaati lay in his former princely estate of Niskashi.

He was deeply perturbed to see the once prosperous lands now engulfed in an air of despair and pathos. The entry of the mining mafia had altered the landscape a few years ago. Sona Ghaati is rich in minerals, but residents live in abject misery, a typical poverty paradox! The mining magnates lead opulent lifestyles as the landowners struggle for two square meals and safe drinking water.

"When the land and livelihood of poor people are snatched, they merely become footnotes in history books, whereas unfortunate incidents happening with celebrities or powerful persons get instantly translated into national crises.What a travesty!!! When will we start judging incidents on the same footing, irrespective of the people they befall?"He wondered.

He was now walking in the forest area as his thoughts got interrupted by the melodious koel and the symphony of water bouncing off the rocks from the nearby waterfall. The innocence of Koel and the free-spirited falling water in tandem reminded him of his childhood. Suddenly, he felt a lump in his throat as he remembered his friend Victor, who had introduced him to nature's orchestra in the babbling streams and gushing waterfalls.

As he was crossing a discarded open mine, childhood memories came alive. Maharaja Shakti Shubhankar's erstwhile opulent palace, its tastefully decorated rooms and the magically ornate ambience soaked in elegant magnificence all began flashing in front of his eyes. The ethereal edifice, influenced by the Western Gothic Style, pointed arches, and vaulted ceilings made the palatial mansion look like a towering beauty resting in the lap of majestic lush green lawns.

It was the rainy season he loved the most when the droplets dared to touch his outstretched hand from the window, the only time when something happened in his life without the Maharaja's permission.

Being a royal scion, Kamtej had the advantage of a luxurious life provided by his father, Maharaja Shakti Shubhankar, who was a complete advisory directorate by himself. His unending saga of 'I Me-Minc' had a mix of self-consciousness, morality and autofiction. Many times, Kamtej felt that it was an attempted hypnosis directed at him, with narratives reeking of edits and modifications suiting Maharaja's palette.

He wanted to be the robotic fulcrum around which everything revolved. Completely devoid of emotions or feelings, Maharaja had laid standard operating procedures for everything, including his own son's thought process! "Isn't he a control freak," young Kamtej wondered.

But when has life followed the directed plans even if ordained by the king? Each person writes his own destiny at his own pace. As Kamtej grew up, he could see that it was getting difficult to fit into his father's scheme of things. His father often put the blame on the generation gap. But was it the only reason? "Why are experience and age always deemed superior over all other factors?" He was still looking for answers even after so many years.

Kamtej was fourteen years old when he sought Maharaja's permission for the school expedition trip. He had been there a few times earlier also, but the royal guards always accompanied him. He was not allowed to run around or climb trees. Playing games was out of question. Just a stroll around the area was permitted, and then back to the car. So going on a trip with his classmates was like a dream come true, but only if his request was acceded to!

To his utter surprise, Maharaja nodded with a slight smile. An excited Kamtej could not sleep the whole night. There were many cars in the palace, but he had never experienced a bus ride. The twelfth of February was one of the brightest mornings of his life. He finished his breakfast and raced towards the palace gate for the school bus.

To his utter shock, it was the usual car which took him to the school every day. Oh no, he protested! "I will go with my classmates on the bus." He ran towards his father's study. His steps grew slower as he approached Maharaja's study room. Maybe his heart was aware of the response.

He could hear Maharaja shouting at the gardener." How dare you think that a servant's son can read from the books of the royal scion?" The request for the old books of Kamtej was audacious, and Maharaja immediately fired the gardener.

Kamtej's joyous mood evaporated in thin air. He stood like a statue as if his feet had been rooted to the ground. Then he thought of Victor and other classmates. They must be waiting for him. With tears rolling down his eyes, he turned back and sat in the car. The skies seemed no more cheerful as he wiped his bleary eyes. As instructed by the Maharaja, he was first taken to his regular horse riding sessions, and from there, he was to join his classmates at lunchtime.

His classmates were boisterous as the expedition trip began across the rough terrain. A gentle breeze and a clear blue sky seemed to boost their spirits as none of them ever had a prior chance to visit Maharaja's estate. A few of them started playing football in a seemingly dry river bed close to a discarded open mine. The rest of the boys cheered them from the sides. The teachers were busy taking out the packed breakfast from the bus, which was parked about five hundred metres from the banks of the dry river.

Meanwhile, some water started pouring into the river bed. The boys were thrilled as the cold water trickled their feet. Suddenly, the trickle surged into a flash flood without any warning. Everyone tried running to safety; it was easier for the boys who were closer to the banks. But for those who were caught in the middle of the stream, it was like a living hell. The water level was rising dangerously, and the roar of gushing water suppressed their cries for help. Those on the banks watched in agony as rocks began vanishing in the flooding water.

A few days later, he met the local police Kaptaan at the palace gates, seeking to meet his father. The Kaptaan was a tall, burly fellow with a dark moustache twitching upwards. He bowed slightly and sought forgiveness for his inability to touch the feet of the young scion."I injured my leg in last week's rescue operation at the accident site of a school expedition trip," said the limping Kaptaan.

Kamtej accompanied him to his father's study. Kaptaan knocked at the door, and curt came the reply, "What is it?" "Sir, it is about Victor", said Kaptaan. He was hastily rushed in, and the door slammed instantly.

'Victor', had he heard correctly? Kamtej's heart was pounding heavily. He wanted to listen to the conversation, but eavesdropping was considered not royal! With tears swelling in his eyes and emotions drowning him further, he decided to seek shelter in the garden. It was Mother Nature's lap that gave him solace and comforted him more than any worldly possessions. He hoped the green landscape would assuage his wandering and injured self. Kamtej tried to close his ears, but Victor's cries for help still hounded him.

Why did nature exact vengeance on his friend? Victor was the first child in his snake catcher family to attend formal school. What was his fault? Had the base of the river been reset by reckless mining operations, or was it a result of Maharaja's avarice? Above all, had nature erred or was it a case of mistaken identity?

The loss of his best friend Victor, widened his rift with Maharaja to a point of no return. Kamtej soon developed a nonchalant attitude towards the royalty, and the father-son interactions dwindled to mere customary greetings.

And then, a few months later, it was Maharaja's birthday, wherein Kamtej was supposed to deliver the welcome speech on behalf of his father. The palace was dazzling like a queen as the guests settled in their respective seats. Ustad Wasiullah's melodious shehnai[14] reverberated in the imperial palace, adding to the entire royal treat.

Kamtej got so immersed in the music that he failed to notice Maharaja's entry. As the guests stood up and bowed to the Maharaja, it was a single chair that did not rise.

Maharaja was furious at Kamtej's insubordination. He whispered something in the royal guard's ears, pointing towards his son.

Kamtej was soon summoned to the inner chamber of the palace. He had never been there before. There was a beautiful wall painting, Gold of Kinabalu, in the chamber. As he stood gazing at the painting, the door behind him was slammed shut. Meanwhile, the festive fireworks had begun outside, and here he was, waiting for someone to rescue him from this dark room.

Tired of standing, he looked for a chair and fell down.For few moments, he sat still. "Why have I been locked here?" Then after sometime, he tried to gather himself up, and his hands brushed against some switch kind of thing. Assuming it to be a light switch, he pressed it on. There was a clicking sound, and then the wall moved. He slowly crossed the false wall partition, and suddenly, there was a bright light in the room for a second, and then it became pitch dark.

---

[14] *musical instrument*

As his eyes tried to accustom to this abrupt change in brightness, he soon realised that he was not alone. Something was moving and making strange sounds in the room. Thankfully, there was now some light coming from the dome. He looked in that direction and froze in horror. He was standing near a snake house. It was a huge glass case with different types of snakes. One of them came close to the glass wall and flashed its sharp fangs. Kamtej fainted and fell on the floor.

The next morning, he was packed to a Boarding School and never came back to Niskashi, not even during vacations. Later, he secured a hundred per cent scholarship at the prestigious National Law College and started working part-time to cover his other expenses. Soon, he sent a legal notice to Maharaja Shakti Shubhankar, severing all ties with him.

Tears welled in his eyes as Kamtej stood beneath the mystical grandiose banyan tree with large aerial roots descending into the soil. The plunging knotted roots from its colossal main trunk seemed to bow down to Mother Earth in reverence, while its gigantic branches gave the impression of embracing the cosmos with open arms. The cool breeze of the leaves apparently had a soothing effect as Kamtej recharged his resolve to fight for Sona Ghaati's people under the sacred Ashwath Vriksha[15].

He had many childhood memories of this place and soon was gripped by nostalgia. Niskashi had changed over the years. Ah! The house of Durjan, the dreaded one-eyed sand mafia, has been bulldozed. There were so many stories about him.

---

[15] *knowledge tree*

Kamtej had also heard a few of them in childhood. The local people were petrified of this living terror, and none had the courage to stand up against him. The big cut on his lower right forehead was the brutal highlight of his ferocious face. Kaptaan had once narrated the story of how it happened that fatal night.

Based on a tip-off, the trap was laid by the police force in the forest. The entire area was cordoned off, and the villagers were told not to come out of their houses. Shoot-at-sight orders were issued against Durjan, and soon, the silence of the night was broken by the intermittent sound of gunshots. Villagers were panic-stricken as the next few hours of ensuing gunfire exchange turned to raging balls of fire and lit the sky that moonless night.

The police teams were now circling towards Durjan. Running out of luck, he dashed towards the ancient temple on the hillock and lay at the foot of Goddess Maya. He hoped the police wouldn't enter the temple and lay still for some time. Then he heard the sound of police gumboots.

Luckily for him, the policeman who entered the temple did not notice that a body was lying over the demon that was beneath Goddess Maya's feet. Durjan held his breath as the policeman bowed before the Goddess to seek her blessings. A flower from Goddess's garland fell in his hands, perhaps a signal that his prayers were about to be answered!

"We found Durjan's gun," shouted his teammate. The policeman instantly came out of the temple and sprinted down the hillock in a hurry. Durjan heaved a sigh of relief and began to wriggle free of the ropes on the demon's body. The platform on which he lay was about six feet from the ground. Oblivious to the fact that his wiggling was vibrating the platform, he continued shaking the ropes vigorously in a bid to free himself.

And then, the Shastra (weapon) in Goddess's hand slipped and pierced through his forehead and right eye. Perhaps it was malediction, the Goddess's curse, that made the evil mark on his face. He survived the night, but the satanic token got marked on his face.

As a kid, Kamtej was never allowed to even go near Durjan's house or talk to any of his neighbours. But just like his classmates, he too was curious to see him once. The opportunity came sooner than expected. In the school's fancy dress competition, one of the senior boys decided to dress up as Durjan. He resembled Jack Sparrows from the Pirates of the Caribbean movie that Kamtej saw years later. The uproar of applause from the students was still afresh in his mind.

This portrayal angered the Principal as his stout face turned red, and he called for an immediate explanation from the teacher's panel that had selected this act. The boy's parents, too, were summoned for their poor parenting skills by the Principal. They got a severe dressing down for being careless about their child's grooming. But that did not deter the boy from becoming an instant sensation in the school.

Working under the cover of darkness, the sand mafia led by Durjan left a trail of destruction and tales of devastation for the local populace. Their nefarious and illegal activities were depleting sand (the world's second most consumed natural resource). But was Durjan alone? No, he had created a network of helpful people, and his reign of terror was being patronised by certain lobbies that were busy making huge profits on their seemingly low investments.

Maharaja Shakti Shubhankar was initially reluctant to be a part of the sand mafia alliance. "What's there in the sand," said Kaptaan in a subdued tone. "In spite of you having the mining lease rights, they are already selling sand of your area, right under your nose,albeit illegally.

Currently, both of you are competitors trudging the same road. Whenever your paths cross, seven times out of ten, you lose, and they gain. I think this offer is a blessing in disguise. Durjan is willing to give you a share in profits and is ready to bear the operational risks. So why don't you accept his partnership offer so that you can eat the cake and let him do the dirty work?"

"Okay, but ask them to follow the rules. Mining must be restricted to three metres or ten per cent of the river's width, whichever is less. And yes, no extraction within five hundred metres of any crucial hydraulic structure," Maharaja shouted at Kaptaan.

Little did he realise that acceptance of this proposal was just chink in the armour, and in a few months, Maharaja and Kaptaan became cogs in the wheel of complacency and acquiescence, and their moral compass turned directionless.

The landscape of Sona Ghaati, the golden land was about to change.Was it the the case of "Killing the duck that lays the golden eggs?" Well, none bothered !

Kamtej had been walking for more than two hours now and

was nearing Fauz Maidan when he called his team to prepare the Public Interest Litigation (PIL) on behalf of the people of Sona Ghaati. After all, Article Forty-Eight A of the Constitution calls upon the State to protect and improve the environment and to safeguard the forest and wildlife of the country. Further, the Hon'ble Supreme Court had expanded the meaning of Article Twenty-One and included the right to a wholesome environment as a part of the right to life.

"Ah, there used to be a hospital here."Kamtej stood for a while staring at the ruins, as childhood memories engulfed him once again. Dr Zaidi of this hospital was the most cheerful and energetic person he met as a child. "You are so different from Maharaja. You get annoyed if your patients use Doctor before your name and he gets annoyed if someone forgets to use Maharaja before his name."

He patted Kamtej's cheeks with a broad smile and said in a hushed voice,"I won't disclose it to Maharaja.But tell me, are your frequent stomach aches real?"

Both looked at each other for a few seconds and then laughed aloud.Maharaja entered the room at that very instant and asked, "is he okay? I never heard him laughing so loud."

Yes Maharaja, "Laughter is the best medicine."

He often said, "Shouldn't justice roll down like the everlasting stream of righteousness so that the world becomes a better place to live and the sunshine of fairness is spread in an equitable manner?"

V

The weather had been inclement since the evening of the 12th of March. But it made no difference to Mayuri and Kavya's midnight celebration plan. After all, it was their friendship anniversary; they could not allow the rain to play spoilsport. Mayuri reached their favourite 'All Night Novelty Café' at around 11.45 pm. The café owner accosted her to the reserved table. It was not every day that he had guests like Mamak ji's daughter. "Ensure the best service without any delay," the owner told his staff. Mayuri ordered Kavya's favourite sponge rasgullas at the counter and was tapping merrily on the table as the sweets arrived, beautifully decorated with flowers and candles.

"Oh! You brought it early," she gently reprimanded the waiter, "I told you to bring them when the clock tower strikes twelve." As she spoke, the faint chimes could be heard at a distance. Where are you, my soul sister Kavya? Come what may, you have never been late on this day.

Mayuri dialled her number, but it was coming out of reach. She called the house help, but that, too, went unanswered. Meanwhile, the drizzle outside had turned to a heavy downpour as she sat near the window waiting for Kavya.

She fondly recalled her first meeting with Kavya at Smithsonian Grand Valley boarding school in Buckinghamshire, England, in March 2004. It was the orientation session, and the two eleven-year-olds were seated next to each other. Both seemed to be overwhelmed by the century-old famous surroundings and were anxious as to what lay ahead in store for them. Mayuri offered Kavya her chocolate with a broad smile. Whether it was due to the chocolate or the dimpled smile,hard to say,but a connection was formed between the two instantly.

As luck would have it, they were allotted the same hostel room. Thus began a spirited journey of two young girls, which bloomed beautifully as they grew up away from home. Although they came from diverse backgrounds, both were foodies.They loved vegetarian food. Neither of them could resist a dessert, be it before or after a meal. Their bond was so strong that other students in the school mistook them as real sisters. Beneath their lavish lifestyles and expensive clothing lay two simple girls with hearts of gold.

Kavya often spoke about Aunt Nikki, who was her late mother Kadambari's bestie. She had lost her mother in a tragic car accident in London when she was just a toddler. Shocked by her friend's death, Aunt Nikki had decided to remain single and raised Kavya as her own child.

It was their final day at college. Kavya was a bit upset as she had not received any letters from Aunt Nikki for about a month now. "Maybe she did not want to disturb you during exams," Mayuri said in a bid to comfort her. "Hey, you two are still here? Let's go to the canteen and join our friends," said the Class Prefect Vinnie.

"Oh! I can't believe that ten years have passed by since we entered this great institution," exclaimed one of the girls. "So true, this place was almost like a family," said another, hugging Kavya. "Let's have a get-together during Convocation," chipped in Mayuri. "Oh, that would be great," said Vinnie as they posed for a group photograph. It seemed everyone was in a mood to sing the school song and shake a leg, adding to the fun and frolic.

"The warden wants to see you," said the messenger to Kavya. "Wait, I will come with you,: said Mayuri, and both sprinted towards the warden's room.

Kavya rarely spoke about her family in college. Her mother, Kadambari, was a princess but had been banished by her royal family. She then moved to London, where Kavya was born. The news spread like wildfire amongst the aristocratic elites that the child had been born out of wedlock. The princess was unmarried and had been in London for only six months. Well, there aren't limitations to conjectures, as many chronicles, as many minstrels.

"Your Aunt sent this packet a few days ago," said the warden, "She had called me over the phone and requested to deliver the packet to you only after the exams." Both friends were ecstatic as they opened it hurriedly. There was a diary, some investment documents and a letter inside it.

Dear Kavya,

This could be my last letter as I am counting my final days. Doctors have also given up hope. You often asked about your mother. I didn't have the courage to tell you earlier. But I think you have a right to know the truth. SP was her biggest mistake. Your mother was unlucky as she relied on those who were unworthy of her trust.

Although she breathed her last in London, her self-esteem had been battered long ago at Angira. But her fighter spirit helped Kadambari brave the emotional trauma, the extreme feeling of vulnerability from her past that refused to go away. She chose you above everything and paid a heavy price for her decision. Even in her death, justice was denied.

Many times, I asked Kadambari, What if I could have prevented SP's entry into her life? What if I had been there on the day he proposed to her in Angira? And Kadambari used to just look at me silently. None of us had any answers. Life is tough, we all know. But I feel it was cruel to my best friend. She was such a nice and caring human being, yet the people close to her were neither nice nor caring towards her. She deserved a better life.

I have bequeathed all my properties to you in the will (lawyers will take care of it). Spread your wings and conquer the world, my child and shine as a star always.

With lots of love,

Nikki.

With trembling hands, she opened the diary, which had the handmade drawing of Gold of Kinabalu orchid on the first page. "It's mom's diary," she hugged it close to her throbbing heart. She was shattered by the devastating revelation of the ignominy that her mother had to face. Tears welled in her eyes as she leaned against the wall.

"Your aunt passed away peacefully in sleep last night," said the warden. She would have collapsed had it not been for

Mayuri's arm. Aunt Nikki was the pillar of strength in her life. Today, she felt like being orphaned again. The agony of not being there with Aunt Nikki in her last moments was too much to bear.

Mayuri tried assuaging her bestie's grief, but she was inconsolable. Unable to bear her friend's sufferings, Mayuri spoke to her father, and it was on his insistence they decided to leave London and come back home. Mamak supported Kavya wholeheartedly and asked her to stay at their house till she got better. After a year, when she shifted to her own villa, Mamak came personally to see her off.

Mayuri stood as a rock behind her friend, and soon, Kavya's entrepreneurial ventures took the nation by storm. Her expertise in connecting the dots from village artisans to global audiences led to remarkable successes in her journey. Her desire to be the change agent fuelled her to push the limits, and the Youngest Female Entrepreneur award was just the beginning, and soon many laurels followed.

It had not been easy for Kavya to track SP. How would she know that a theatre artist of the early nineties has now turned into a shark? "Rather, calling him an artist is a disgrace," she told Mayuri."He is a fraudster, a conman who killed my mother."

She began with Angira and then slowly picked up the clues on the run. Mayuri stood by her through thick and thin and once proposed the idea of taking help from her resourceful father, Mamak. But Kavya stood firm against any outside help. "It is my fight, and I will make him pay for his sins."

It was now one thirty am of their friendiversary night, and still no response from her! Mayuri was getting more and more worried. Sensing something amiss, she wanted to rush immediately to her friend's bungalow. But her driver was a bit apprehensive as the streets were full of water and cautioned her, "Madam, please wait for some time. The street lights are not working, and the rain is also pouring relentlessly."

A notification rang on her mobile, a high tide alert at two a.m. With Kavya's residence so close to the ocean, she knew that it wouldn't be possible for her to reach there soon. Fearing for her friend's safety, she then called the Police Commissioner, shared Kavya's address and requested him to send a police team immediately.

She kept praying inside the café for her wellbeing and dashed to her bestie's residence at around quarter to three in the morning. The street lights were thankfully working now as her driver manoeuvred his way through the water-filled roads.

Police sirens were buzzing in the area, and the bungalow had been cordoned off by the time Mayuri reached there. The police were not letting anyone in. "I am Mamak Vragji's daughter," shouted Mayuri, raising her voice above the din. Immediately, the way was cleared, and the police in charge greeted her with folded hands. "She is my best friend; find her," said Mayuri in the authoritative tone of her politician father.

Her umbrella flew away as the strong gales pounded furiously against the trees. With the rumbling thunderous skies and indignant winds smacking against the window panes in tandem, it seemed as if nature had unleashed its wrath.

The police rang the doorbell, but there was no response. "The keys are beneath the third flower pot on the right," said

Mayuri loudly. As they opened the main door, the lobby looked spotlessly clean.

Kavya's friends often teased, that her house looked like a luxurious hotel! Prima facie, there weren't any apparent signs of forced entry, theft or robbery. The exquisitely handcrafted artefacts, the signature collection of art paintings on the walls and the Flora Danica tableware; everything was intact and precisely at its place.

The forensics team began their work in the lobby. A nervous Mayuri accompanied the police to Kavya's bedroom, which was locked from inside. The police knocked on the door as Mayuri called her friend but to no avail. She continued praying, but somewhere in her heart, a fear was lurking. "Call the locksmith," said the police officer. "Sir, he is stuck on the way due to bad weather," informed his junior.

Mayuri requested the police to break open the door forcibly without wasting any more time. Sensing that it was a high-profile case and moreover, how could anyone dare to decline Mamak ji's daughter's request? The police officer ordered his men to break open the door of the bedroom.

As the door flung open, Mayuri fainted, seeing her best friend lying motionless on the right side of the king-size bed. The doctor, who had arrived just then, looked for her pulse and shook his head in negative.

The room was absolutely in order, with no signs of struggle whatsoever. The window panes were open, and a glass of aam panna [16]was kept on the window sill. The glass was full, and perhaps Kavya had not drunk it. The forensics team began rummaging through the room for any suicide note and/or any other evidence.

"Two chargers were plugged in near the bedside table, but her laptop and iPhone were conspicuously missing!"

As the forensic team members were collecting the glass from the window sill, one of them shouted loudly. All the members drew close to the window; the house help's still body lay on the ground. But why would someone kill her?

Two members of the forensics team were asked to check the area near her, but due to heavy rains, the possibility of finding footprints or tyre marks seemed remote.

"Sir, there is a CCTV camera on the front door," informed one of the policemen. They all rushed to watch the footage of the last evening. The monitor displayed 12th March, six p.m., as a delivery boy rang the doorbell with a big gift packet and a bouquet of Gold of Kinabalu orchids. He handed it over to the house help and went back within two minutes. After that, no activity was reported by the cameras.

But where was the gift? Police did not find the gift box or orchids inside the house. Mayuri was again looking at the CCTV footage and, seeing the flowers, mumbled, "Oh! They were on Kavya's bucket list. They had cast a spell on her since she saw them at an exhibition in the school, and perhaps it symbolised a connection with her mother. She

---

[16] *raw mango drink*

loved the long sweeping petals of the rare flowers and called them the outstretched arms of the dancers," sighed Mayuri. One thing was certain: the sender of the gift was not a stranger.He knew Kavya well.

The morning session of share market on 13th March was not favourable as the death of Kavya caused a negative sentiment on PENAK's shares. To add to its woes, the US Federal Reserves announced a rise in interest rates by fifty basis points. The markets tumbled further,taking PENAK's shares down with them.

Kavya's death added to the hype around the first hearing of the paternity suit case filed against Shyam Pradosh. There was a huge media contingent outside the courtroom. The court compound was abuzz with various theories, including his probable confession in the court today.

The media's curiosity also lay in the defendant's Lawyer, Mugdha Pradosh, daughter of Shyam Pradosh. She was an excellent lawyer in her own right, with or without her father's name. She had established her credentials at an early age with a high winning percentage and had carved a niche for herself in the legal world. For her, the Pradosh surname was a burden, and she rarely used it.

The surname was botheration, but when it came to her father's name, it all turned to humongous admiration.He was her role model, a complete family man."Media reports against him,are nothing but a figment of oppostion's imagination." She was very close to her father, and the two shared a very strong bond. Her papa was the best, and for SP, no daughter could ever be better than Mugdha.

Meanwhile, the media personnel were waiting for the potboiler to unfold in the courtroom with the half-sisters taking on each other. 'Mugdha Vs Kavya' headline was ready to be telecast. Alas! Kavya's death changed the scene near the courtroom compound. As far as the law was concerned, with the sole plaintiff's demise, the suit's not abated if the right to sue survives. It can be continued by the heirs and legal representatives of the deceased plaintiff.

Disbelief, incoherence and, above all, loneliness gripped Mayuri as she accompanied her bestie to the hospital. The vibrant diva had been covered in a white bed sheet, a colour that Kavya hated the most. "What will I do without you? Why did you go away so soon? Please come back Kavya," wailed Mayuri as tears rolled down her cheeks.

The ambulance screeched to a halt, interrupting her chain of thoughts. They had reached the Pradosh Hospital. Intense pain and grief tormented Mayuri as she hugged her bestie tightly for the last time. Wasn't it a cruel irony that Kavya's body had been brought into the hospital owned by Shyam Pradosh?

Mayuri strongly held the railings, but her feet seemed unable to bear the heart's weight as she saw the body being taken for autopsy. Mayuri and Kavya were inseparable; their lives were intricately woven around each other. "Then why did she take this extreme step, and that too on our friendiversary," wept Mayuri inconsolably.

The police had their task well cut. Right now, they seemed to have no evidence, akin to looking for a needle in a haystack. But going by their past experience, they knew that by sticking their fingers in the hay for a long, there was a possibility of finding something. Of course, they also ran the risk of getting pricked in the process.

In the first instance ,the crime scene pointed towards suicide rather than murder.But there was no suicide note in her room.She was supposed to meet Mayuri at Novelty Café in few hours for celebrating their friendiversary. Suddenly, why would she take this extreme step ?

What if,it was a murder? Kavya was a public figure. She was an established and wealthy businesswoman. Maybe, jealousy was the motive of her killers. Maybe someone close, or an insider. Could it be a case of supari killing[17]? But then ,why was the maid killed? Had she seen the killer?

The police had faced such situations in the past also when their investigation led to fingers being pointed at famous people in the society, with some harrowing secrets coming out. The police had seen unpredictable twists and turns in such cases. Were the skeletons in the closet about to tumble?

---

[17] *contract killing*

VI

Numbed by the news of Kavya's death, Kraman kept staring blankly at the window in front of him. Were these happenings a part of a jigsaw puzzle, or was he caught in a web of unrelated incidents? He needed clarity, but there were no easy answers around him. So he decided to get some fresh air and moved towards the nearby beach; it always helped.

As he stood there for Surya Namaskar, he could see the rising sun and against that magnificent background were fishermen's boats returning back to the shore with their loads of fish, lobsters, crabs, prawns, etc. On the benches along the walls, a few old fishermen were seated with their hands folded on their knees. Some of them seemed to be gazing at the sea while others were smoking beedi.

The waves seemed to be drenching the sand graciously as they gently crawled to the shore and, while receding, formed interesting artistic patterns on the sand. The flax golden beach had few tourists, and that gave Kraman the luxury of watching the horizon leisurely. The thin seam where the canopy of blue sky and the sea intertwined into each other to form a golden line looked mesmerising. He would have loved to gaze continuously had it not been for ……

Vada pav tapri on the beach. Kraman grinned like a Cheshire

cat. The spicy potato patties dipped in besan[18] batter were deep-fried in hot oil, and he could not resist ordering them. As the shopkeeper was busy packing the vada pav along with green chillies and sweet & green chutney in a newspaper, Kraman was impatient like a kid. He hastily took his first bite as the crisp crust to its soft filling literally melted into his mouth. It was an irresistible gastronomical delight. Aha! It's heavenly! "Abhari ahe Kaka, vada pav khoop chaan ahe (*Thanks Kaka, vada pav is very good*)."

He was looking for a dustbin to throw the newspaper which held his delicious vada pav till a few moments ago. Then his eyes fell on the photo and the caption in the paper - WANTED DURJAN (Dead or Alive). Curiously, he looked closely at the photograph. It was hazy, but he looked similar to Lal Kunwar in the plane. Only the outfits were completely different. The man in the photo was wearing local attire - dhoti, kurta and a pagdi, unlike the suit, hat and sunglasses worn by Lal Kunwar.

Durjan is wanted by the police for his involvement in illegal mining! Could the limping Lal Kunwar from the plane be involved with the mafia? How could it be possible! Suddenly, a football hit his head. A few youngsters in Lionel Messi T-shirts were practising on the beach. "Sorry, bro," said one of them, even as Kraman returned the ball with a smile.

As Kraman entered the hotel, the receptionist wished him, "Sir, there is a gift for you. I will get it delivered to your room soon." "Don't bother with the formalities," he said.

---

[18] *gram flour*

He picked up the small gift box and moved towards the capsule lift. Once inside the room, he looked closely at the box. It had a number lock mechanism. "So, this is the gift my sponsor was referring to," thought Kraman as he punched 15081947 (Indian Independence Day in dd-mm-yyyy format as instructed). Kraman keenly looked inside the box; it had an envelope with an invitation card for the Rainbow Conclave ceremony on the fourteenth of March at 6 p.m. "Is that all?" wondered Kraman.

He took out the first envelope from his bag to recheck if it had any more information. As he held both the envelopes together, the first one fell on the table, and the sand-like material spilt out of it. "Oh!" he exclaimed loudly before collecting the same and putting it back in the second envelope.

But wait, there seemed to be something on the backside of the invitation card. He held it against the bulb in the room. Some words appeared, but they were not readable. His scout training on invisible ink came in handy as he rushed to get the hair dryer from the washroom and put it on maximum heat. Once the paper got heated, the words became clearer,

One for three and three for one,

Is it a Panch Mukhi rerun?

Shark Kothi is camouflage green,

Someone needs to warn the queen.

Wine is old, but the bottle is new,

The Omniscient Ocean knows what is true.

Rainbow Conclave, 13th March, eleven a.m.

I will be there at gate number seven.

Now, what was that supposed to mean? "Rainbow Conclave was scheduled for the evening of 14th March. Then why am I being called at the venue on 13th March at eleven a.m.?"

Suddenly, there was a huge sound, as if some tyre had burst, followed by an explosion. He tried to look out of the window, but all he could see was billowing smoke. There was another louder explosion, and it seemed nearer this time. Instinctively, he put the second envelope in the pocket and dashed out of the room. There were other guests, too, rushing towards the stairs with shrieking sounds of help. What the hell was happening?

"Everything is fine, Sir, nothing to panic," said Chris, the hotel manager, with a forced smile on his face. "There was a gas cylinder cart which exploded near the hotel. The boundary wall of the hotel has been damaged. As a precautionary measure, we are getting all the rooms sanitised, and very soon, you can return to your respective rooms. Please relax and enjoy the complimentary food and beverages till then." The announcement seemed to lighten up the mood of the guests.

But Kraman was thinking: "first the hand drawn map by Shlok and now this riddle; there seemed to be some connection between the two. TECHSIKA, Nabinagar and the forests of Sona Ghaati; what could be the link between them? Was this the story that Shlok was pursuing at Nabinagar, which led to his disappearance?"

It took more than an hour, but when Kraman reached his room, it was spotlessly clean, as if nothing had happened. He started packing his bags, but something was amiss. He rechecked his things. Ah, Suchita didi's envelope, the first one in which his tickets were sent, was not there on the table.

"But it was an empty envelope with maybe a few granules of sand-like material. Why would someone come to steal an old envelope when my iPhone, laptop, and wallet everything was on the table itself? The hotel was on high alert due to the explosion; an outsider could not have dared to come to my room."

Could it be the room service people? Nope, the envelope had nothing precious inside it, and moreover, Moksha was a reputed hotel. Its staff members' conduct was beyond reproach. He rechecked his pockets. The second envelope with the invitation card and sand-like material was tucked there in his left pocket. He took it out and looked at it one more time before keeping it in his backpack safely.

Was the intruder looking for the sand-like material? Taking all the trouble for searching his backpack and the room made no sense to Kraman.

The phone's ringtone broke the silence in his hotel room. It was Nancy confirming his arrival. "I will be sending a car tomorrow evening to pick you up," she said. "Thanks, Nancy, but I plan to catch up with friends today. Don't worry, I will be at the function venue on time," he replied.

His eyes were still fixated on the riddle at the backside of the invitation card. In this digital age, why would someone use invisible ink to convey a message? Either the sender was ignorant about the latest technology, or else he was so smart that he did not want to leave any digital footprint?

"Well, in a couple of hours, the identity of the mysterious sender would be unveiled. He must have pulled some strings to get my name as the official invitee from my media house. How else would a junior like me attend such a huge event?"

"Is Shlok at Nabinagar? I hope he is safe," said Kraman aloud. But why is he not responding to my messages? It has been more than a month now. A police complaint was also filed after his disappearance, but nothing came out of it. There weren't any ransom calls to his family either.

"Could Dr Chandrasi's unofficial visit to Nabinagar and the flight UV 432 hijack be related to Shlok's disappearance?"

The mention of Panch Mukhi in the riddle confounded him. "Is it a pointer to some historical antecedent? The wounds of the tragic night had still not healed. Is someone planning revenge? But why wait for so many years?"

"The venue of Rainbow Conclave, being a couple of kilometres away from Tarulia village, is perhaps not a mere coincidence. Something's cooking ! Whosoever is behind this wants to make a grand statement. That's why he chose this venue, and with so many VIPs in Nabinagar, his plan is bound to get massive attention." Kraman was sure.

It was a local holiday, and hence, the guards were a bit surprised to see Dr Chandrasi. "Good Morning," Madam, they wished her while opening the outer gate. Chandrasi drove her white WagonR inside the campus. "Is anyone else also expected, Madam?" Asked the main guard courteously. She smiled and said, "I know it is the thirteenth of March. All of you can have a break of three hours for the Naru Puja. I will activate the automated entry system during that period."

The guards were more than happy to hear that and thanked her profusely. As Chandrasi entered the main building of the satellite office NODO Nabinagar, she activated the automated entry system. It was a highly secure system wherein, once activated, the whole building turned into a fortress. Only she could change it to manual command, and that too, only from a specified terminal in the building. In her absence, the automated entry system could be disabled only by the Beta codes of Central Command.

"Madam is so nice; she has given leave to her driver also. She was working till late at night yesterday and came to the office early today. Grateful to have such a boss who is working herself on a holiday but does not want to bother her subordinates. May God fulfil her dreams," said the guards gratuitously. As the skies were growing darker, they doubled their speed lest the rains drenched them.

Dr Chandrasi was watching the guards from the window. Just then, her cell beeped, 'team reaching in ten minutes'. She rechecked the information on her tab. Her security team had sent the pattern of attempted data breaches. The data was accurate, yet seemingly unusual. As she wrote down the dates when maximum attempts were made, they looked familiar, as if they were following a pattern. A glance at her desktop calendar, and she smiled impishly. All the dates were on Purnima[19]! Was it a coincidence or insider information?

---

[19] *full moon night*

Every Purnima night, the servers used to be reset and new codes were generated. It happened at a specific time, but very few people were privy to this secret information. This practice had been initiated by Lenkesh, her predecessor at the main office of NODO Lalpura.

Lenkesh was technically sound and academically brilliant, and his cabin was called the water kingdom by his subordinates, wherein he was the undisputed king. A complete workaholic by choice, he would stay for weeks at NODO researching the ocean.

Dr Chandrasi had been his fan in the past but severed all relations with him once she came to know of his illegal dealings and shady associations with the private mining companies. He was a genius turned rogue who had smeared the organisation's image. Dr Chandrasi shuddered as she recalled the shocking events of that catastrophic night in December 2004.

Decades ago, NODO's journey began at Lalpura with the pledge of 'serving the nation till our last breath'. The building and the surroundings changed over the years, but the shroud of secrecy remained intact. It looked like a typical government office building from the outside.

But it was more than sixty-five feet underground, with the servers and the coolants dug deep and secure. Its automated air ventilation system was capable of changing the air in the facility thrice every hour. It had an underground generator room designed to support 24 MW of backup generator power along with the underground fuel area that could hold 75000 gallons of diesel. There were layers of security, and in case of level two being breached, the system would shut down automatically.

In such a scenario, the backup servers at the hot site had to be activated. It was a three-tier authorization. Firstly, the passcodes had to be loaded into the system, and then it required iris authentication of Chief Scientist Dr Chandrasi. As a defence research organisation, they had a few ghost members who seemingly did their nine-to-five boring office jobs in various parts of the country. The final authorization was given by one of them for the restart of the original servers. Who would be the lucky authorizer was finalised by the dark net machine kept in the secure precincts of the National Intelligence Unit in the capital.

These members did not know each other; rather, the majority of NODO staff was ignorant about the existence of such members in their organisation. These ghost members were recruited through a rigorous process after a lot of screenings. Dr Chandrasi called them crème de la crème (best of the best). These ghosts sprang to life only in case of emergencies. Once the authorization was done, the original servers came to life caudally.

Her team had arrived. She quickly went to the specific terminal and put the gate entry system to manual. The cars moved swiftly inside, and the members alighted in a hurry. The identities, as well as the outcome of this classified meeting, needed to be under wraps.

NODO had enemies like the sand mafia and illegal miners in this area, but their attack style was shoot and scoot. They had never struck in such a detailed manner in the past. Moreover, their previous attacks had been limited to underwater operations. But today's charge was a sort of synchronised Air-Land battle. Although the ransomware attack had been intercepted and neutralised, it was still an ominous signal.

Were the attacks on her and NODO a ploy to divert attention? She needed to unearth the truth soon as the big day was approaching fast.

"NODO is going to unleash its fury to decimate the enemy," she said aloud as the team began the deliberations.

"The technical details look good, and there should not be last-minute hiccups," quipped a member.

"Yes," said Dr Chandrasi. The programme is running on schedule, and the fifteenth of March is going to be remembered as a red letter day when Nabinagar will secure its rightful place in history. The fructification of our years of research is so near, and together, we will fulfil the promises made to our people. Protection of TECHSIKA is paramount, and we will keep it safe, she declared.

Part II

Flashback —

Every present hath a past....

VII

The year was 1983, when SP was still known as Shyam Pradosh. He was the eldest of five siblings living in a thatched hut at Sumerukhed village. His parents worked in the field as daily wagers. Shyam Pradosh and his family were leading an incognito life just like hordes of people around them. Family's meagre earnings were often gobbled by the local liquor shop, where his father was a daily visitor. He would come home every night drunk as a skunk and beat his mother till she fell unconscious. Shyam Pradosh was used to seeing this in his neighbourhood, too and as a child, he often thought that drinking and wife beating were the primary functions of a man.

Neither the women protested, nor the men relented. What surprised Shyam Pradosh was that even the mother-in-law made no effort to control their son. As a youngster, he often wondered, " whether the problem lay with the menfolk who beat their wives mercilessly or with their mothers who did not teach their sons to treat the womenfolk as equals?" In the mornings, his baba would be completely normal and ask for forgiveness. Sometimes, he promised to quit drinking, but it never happened.

Shyam Pradosh was eighteen when his father passed away. That morning, the entrance results had been declared. He had secured a seat in the illustrious HK College and was so excited that he ran with the newspaper to his father. "Baba, I got selected," he shouted with joy. His father snatched the newspaper and tore it down. Tossing it into the chulha's[20] fire, he slapped his son. "From where the hell did you get the money for filling this useless form?"

Tears swelled in his eyes as Shyam Pradosh walked out; else, the beatings would have continued. He was wandering in the nearby forest when his friend Lalu came looking for him. He shouted from a distance, "Something's happened to your baba." He rushed home on Lalu's cycle. His father was vomiting blood. The doctor had warned him multiple times, but baba did not stop drinking. Even in his last moments, his eyes were not looking for his wife or kids, but they were searching for a sip from the liquor bottle.

While lighting the pyre, amidst his siblings' cries, Shyam Pradosh was neither grievous nor had any feeling of loss. Actually, deep down in his heart, he had a sense of relief, as if a problem had been resolved. But as the eldest child, the family's responsibilities now lay on his shoulders. His mother had become quite frail and, many a time, needed help to even walk properly. He abandoned his college dream and decided to work in the paddy fields.

A fortnight later, when he was taking his mother to the dispensary, there was a lot of commotion near the Gram Sabha Building. A new board was hung over it, Kaushal Vikas Kendra (Skill Development Centre). Even in the dispensary, everyone seemed excited with the news of big officers arriving from the city today.

---

[20] *hearth*

"The National Oceanic Defence Organisation (NODO) is organising an essay writing competition, and the winner will get a monthly stipend of five hundred rupees for a year," said Teju Chacha. He was the only person in the village with a graduate degree. Most of the youngsters did not even know his real name. Perhaps the name Teju had been given as he was tej (*brilliant*) in studies!

Shyam Pradosh had never been a bright student but was blessed with a sharp mind and good writing skills. Having studied on mats in the village school under the trees with old torn books, he was aware of the hardships of life lurking around the corner. "Five hundred rupees a month could ease almost all his troubles," thought Shyam Pradosh. "Don't worry; you will do good," said Teju Chacha, patting his back.

In the afternoon, a colourful shamiana[21] was set up in front of the Gram Sabha building, where most of the villagers had assembled out of curiosity. And for the children, it was sheer magic to see the cars and jeeps in their village. Of course, vehicles arrived in the village during elections, too, but that happened only once in five years. So, for the kids, it was a bonanza as they waited outside the village for the vehicles to arrive. The fumes emanating from the vehicles and the smell of diesel in the air excited the kids as they ran behind them! Of course, on the rickety, potholed roads, the kids easily matched the speed of these vehicles.

The village head welcomed the Chief Guest Lenkesh and garlanded him. It was here that Shyam Pradosh first saw

---

[21] *tent*

Lenkesh. He had already submitted his essay along with other youngsters in the village and was about to go home.

"Sir, we have collected the essays and will send the results in a week," said his manager. But Lenkesh insisted on declaring the result on the spot itself. "Why this sudden change," thought the manager and then he saw Lenkesh eyeing the youngsters playing football on the other side of the ground. The manager smiled and said, "There are about twelve essays, and it will take about an hour to go through them. Why don't you join the boys till then?"

Perhaps he was waiting for this comment as he took out his coat, loosened the tie and was soon dribbling the football along with the local boys. He looked like any neighbourhood guy as Shyam Pradosh watched him in awe. Lenkesh's personality seemed magnetic, forcing him to stay on the ground near the tent.

Later in the programme, the anchor called for questions from the audience. Only one hand was raised. "So, whom do you want to answer your question?" The anchor asked. Shyam Pradosh pointed his finger towards Lenkesh. There was a pin-drop silence in the crowd. The village head's face grimaced with anger. "What good is this drunkard's son?" A visibly amused Lenkesh took the mike and told him to ask the question. "Sir, when you were of my age, what was your aspiration," he asked a bit hesitantly?

"I wanted to be Lenkesh", pat came the unabashed reply. The men on the dais looked at Lenkesh, with admiration. What a confidence! "And what do you want to be, young man," asked Lenkesh sportingly. "Sir, I, too, want to be Lenkesh." The village crowd was stunned, but when they saw the people on the dais smiling and clapping, they, too, joined the chorus.

Soon, the results were ready. "And the winner of today's competition is Shyam Pradosh!" Announced Lenkesh. Shyam Pradosh touched his feet with gratitude as Lenkesh patted his back and said, "Congratulations! But you have a long name. I think SP suits your personality more. A new beginning awaits you. Go make the most out of it."

He cried a lot while leaving Sumerukhed. There were tears of sorrow for leaving his family behind and that of joy for his new life ahead. He had never been to a city before. Many things changed for SP. Soon, he graduated with flying colours and got a good consulting job with a decent salary at Angira. But he was not satisfied and wanted more money, albeit the easy way. In his quest for easy money, he forgot the old saying, "When there's muck, there's brass". For him, the decent salary was like peanuts. He needed lots of money if only some godsend miracle happened.

It had been almost nine years since he left Sumerukhed. One day, while reading the morning newspaper, he saw a cricket quiz on the sports page. As he looked for details, he was overjoyed to see that the winner would receive an all-expenses paid trip for the India-England ODI (One Day International) at RoopNagar.

Being a cricket buff, he filled in the right answers and dropped the response at the collection box of the local newspaper office. There were many forms with all correct entries, so the organisers decided to have a lucky draw to decide the winner. As luck would have it, SP won the lucky draw and soon was on the way to watch the sixth India-

England One Day International, live at Sarvesh Kalia stadium, RoopNagar. Little did he realise that the event was about to change his life.

As Princess Kadambari entered the stadium along with her father, the entire stadium erupted with joy, and many of the spectators stood up as a mark of respect. The Royals waved to the crowd before settling in the VIP arena of the stadium. The English openers seemed to be enjoying their batting as the scoreboard showed one hundred twenty-one without loss. It was the first ball of the twenty-second over, and the English Captain hit a straight six over the bowler's head. Incidentally, it landed in the safe hands of SP, sitting in the stands.

The second ball was also hit in a similar fashion, but the batsman had a brain fade and did not notice that the Indian captain had placed a fielder near the side screen at the straight boundary. The shot this time had a little less power in it, and the fielder in the deep took a brilliant catch. The elated crowd roared with joy. It was at this point that the game completely turned on its head. With their in-form captain gone and spin being introduced in the attack, the English batsmen could not offer much resistance. Rest of the side soon crumbled under the Indian spin attack.

Later, Princess Kadambari sent him an autographed box of chocolates during the drinks break. Perhaps she considered his catch in the stands to be lucky for the Indian team. He stood up and bowed in her direction, fully aware of the fact that the distance between his seat and the VIP arena existed in the stadium as well as in the outside world.

India won the match by four wickets and, to SP's delight, his favourite batsman Mohd. Amiruddin was bestowed the Man of the Match award. He had smashed a blazing century, cracking four sixes and six fours all over the ground and most importantly, his winning innings deflated England's chances of levelling the series. India won the series 4-2.

As luck would have it, he again crossed paths with Princess Kadambari at a café in Angira main market. Initially, it was just a brief hello, and then the conversations began to flow. She had recently joined Angira University under the MBA student exchange programme for two semesters. Although they belonged to two different worlds, love for theatre was a strong common factor. SP enjoyed acting; he loved the arch lights, and she became a huge fan of his plays.

Kadambari was so mesmerised by his acting on the stage that she mistook the reel for real. She did not realise that this interest in theatre was turning into affection for SP. By the time the realisation dawned upon her, it was too late!

SP picked up her naivety and played his part well. He narrated stories about his Rajwada and the fabulous palatial life. She fell for it and began to believe that SP was her prince charming and a perfect life partner. It was on his insistence that they decided not to make their relationship public till he broke the news to his family.

"My best friend Nikki is coming from London next week. Oh, I am so happy," she said in a joyous mood. That afternoon, he accompanied Kadambari to the orchid exhibition which had an assortment of playful blue orchids, harmonious green orchids, royal purple orchids and elegant lavender orchids spread beautifully.

Being a working day, there wasn't much rush at the exhibition. The exotic and graceful orchids with their geometric-shaped petals bore pure, luxurious looks. But it was the Gold of Kinabalu orchids which stole Kadambari's heart. She was awestruck the moment her eyes fell on the rare orchid.

SP seized the opportunity and bent on his knees to propose. It was hard to say if Kadambari was swept by the Gold of Kinabalu orchids or SP's proposal. Her face blushed and turned red as she immediately said 'YES'. His happiness knew no bounds.

"My parents have invited us to Rajwada," announced SP as soon as they reached Kadambari's place at Angira. The first thing that she wanted to do was to share this news with her bestie, Nikki. She had so far not disclosed her fondness for SP to anyone, including Nikki, on his insistence. "She is going to kill me," said Kadambari in a lighter mood.

"Nikki is your best friend, and she will understand," said SP, "I think it would be better to share this news with her in person when she arrives next week. Tomorrow afternoon, our official entourage will be here to take us to Rajwada. Our whole palace is being decorated for your arrival. A special puja has been arranged for us at our Kuldevi temple, as it is our age-old tradition wherein new members of the family seek blessings before going to Rajwada."

"What should I wear tomorrow? It is such an important day in my life." Kadambari took out her diamond sets. "Are they good enough:" She asked. "Oh, they seem to have a crust of dirt on it," said SP. "I have a friend who owns a jewellery chain. They have been making jewellery for our family for generations. Tomorrow morning, I will get all these polished. Don't worry, I will purchase some new jewellery and dresses too," said SP.

Kadambari had no idea that SP had seen the bundle of notes in her bag. She put all her jewellery back in the bag. "Ah, just leave the bag on the table," said SP as he drew Kadambari closer to himself.

When she woke up in the morning, SP was not there. As she looked out of the window, her BMW car was also missing. "He might have gone to the jeweller," thought Kadambari, as the bag was also not on the table. She went back to her dreamy world for some more time. Her sleep was interrupted by the phone call. She picked up the phone, "Where are you SP?" She said in a drowsy voice.

"Hey, it's me, Nikki! Are you still sleeping? It is almost noon, lazybones! Get up, and why the hell did you call me SP? And who is he, by the way? Has my voice changed so much?" Nikki asked in jest.

Somewhere in her mind, Kadambari could see that she had been cheated, but hoping against hope, she just wished the doorbell would ring. "SP will be here soon, and we will go to meet his parents," she said to herself. Heart and brain are like two parallel lines of a railway track; they never meet.

It was getting late now, and SP had not yet returned. Kadambari's expectations were receding, as the sun took the final plunge under the horizon. Her worst fears were surfacing: had she been manipulated?

She had never been to his house in Angira and had no idea in which locality he lived. They always met at theatres, exhibitions and, of course, Kadambari's place. He was a good actor who made her believe in his stories. But today, his castle of lies came crashing on her, and she lay bruised and battered.

The person whom she trusted more than herself had vanished without a trace in the air. Was she foolish, or had she been tricked? This question was haunting her.

Her voice was shaking; a pall of loneliness seemed to be sweeping the room. The feeling of having been beguiled was crushing her from inside. The pangs of pain were so excruciating that she was unable to breathe. It was difficult for her to think logically or even coherently as she was engulfed in extreme emotions. She moved towards the window. It was a starless cloudy night. The darkness inside her seemed to merge with it.

It had been a week now with no signs of SP. Kadambari's condition could have worsened had Nikki not preponed her trip to Angira. It was Nikki's healing touch that helped her to stabilise a bit. But she was more worried about the reactions at home. In a fortnight, her exams would be over. She would have to go home and face her family. All hell would break loose once they found out about SP.

For them, the creator of the Universe had cast life in stone. They perceived everything in the realm of black or white only. The possibility of a spectrum of grey-white or a kind of grey-black did not exist for them.

Unfortunately, Raja Sahib came to know of it. Stories have a tendency to spread their wings across borders. Even the thought of a royal princess in love with a commoner was an insult to Raja Sahib. Kadambari was prohibited from joining the morning prayers as a sign of her banishment. Her favourite chair at the dining table was removed, signalling that she was not welcome to dine with the family. Her nightmares had sprung to life.

Then, one fine morning, Raja Sahib called her for arti[22]. Kadambari thought that maybe everything was going to be alright now. All the family members hugged her. Dadi[23] told the cook to prepare mawa kachori[24], ghevar[25] and boondi ke laddoo [26].

"Oh, all my favourites!" Grinned Kadambari as she touched Dadi's feet.

But her happiness did not last long as she saw Raja Sahib moving towards her with the vermillion red chunari[27]. Kadambari had seen it so many times; the chunari symbolised the fixing of engagement. Panditji soon announced that the engagement date had been fixed for next month's purnima.

Kadambari was sitting still as a silhouette against the bustling palace. Her heart was dark as a dead man's eye. "SP cared for my wealth, and my family cared for their honour! With whom should I be angrier, the deceitful SP or my holier-than-thou family?" Unable to bear this pain, she decided to move back

---

[22] *morning prayers*

[23] *Grandmother*

[24] *a popular Rajasthani Mithai where a crunchy sweet crust is filled with sweetened Khoya and lot of nuts.*

[25] *a Rajasthani cuisine disc-shaped sweet made from ghee, flour, and sugar syrup.*

[26] *a ball shaped sweet made by blending fried gram flour drops with sugar syrup.*

[27] *bridal veil,stole*

to her room.

The royal groom was chosen by her father, and he fitted the bill perfectly. Kunwar ji was rich and belonged to a royal family. "What if he was a widower and had a ten-year-old daughter?" It didn't matter to Raja Sahib. At least he was ready to marry Kadambari at such short notice! And none bothered to ask if Kadambari was okay with this proposal.

"She had smiled when Kunwar ji's family sent the wedding gifts," said her aunt. "Kadambari looked so well and fresh at the morning breakfast table," added Dadi. Little did they realise that well-being does not always denote happiness; many a time, it is a mere dialectic between positive and negative.

On her engagement night, Kadambari looked resplendent in a maroon lehenga embellished with diamond trinkets. Ruby studded necklace, along with matching earrings and bracelet, complemented her beauty on the full moon night.

She was the cynosure of the ceremony being held in the midst of Tarana Lake. Everyone looked envious of the groom as the couple walked together to seek the blessings of the elders. Just as the ring ceremony was about to begin, there was some commotion on the stage. "Call the doctor," someone shouted, "Kadambari has fainted."

"She was on a fast today and must have been exhausted. The doctor is looking after her. Don't worry," said Raja Sahib to the groom. There were murmurs in the hall as nearly thirty minutes passed by. "I will go myself and check," he said. As he entered the courtyard, he saw Dadi sitting there, holding her head in her hands. "The auspicious time is about to begin, and you are sitting quietly here?" Raja Sahib was furious, "Where is Kadambari? Is she okay? What did the doctor say?"

Dadi continued sitting there with her head bowed as if she was hiding her face. "Kadambari is not well, you will have to cancel the function," she spoke in a hushed tone. Raja Sahib's face was livid with anger as he spoke to the doctor.

The royal groom did not even wait to speak with Kadambari or at least inquire about her health. He and his ten-year-old daughter hurriedly left the venue along with their guests as if Kadambari was a bad omen. He expected her to be a dutiful wife. She was supposed to become a good mother to his ten-year-old daughter from day one, but had he bothered to ask Kadambari about her expectations of him?

Perhaps he was too self-centred to ponder over that! Or maybe he believed that marriage has an 'I' and not a 'U'. So his 'I' was there intact, and the 'U' for Kadambari never existed. Hence, 'I plus U' evolving into the "US" was out of the question.

The palace, which was buzzing with festivities a little while ago, now wore a deserted look. All the decorative lights and water fountains near Tarana Lake had been switched off. The musicians were wrapping up their instruments. The erstwhile vibrant food court bore a desolate look. Majority of the guests had left.A sudden emptiness now seemed to flow from the magnificent windows and the majestic doors of the bedecked venue. As the full moon hid behind the clouds, the entire venue was engulfed in a hushed silence.

But none could feel the silence and darkness in Kadambari's

heart. She was sitting alone in the room, expecting a family member to come and share her pain.

But they were all busy pointing fingers at Kadambari as if it was entirely her fault. Character vilification soon followed. They were unmindful of her anguish; all they cared for was their societal reputation. What will people say was the common refrain. The family and the society became the self-proclaimed jury, and their verdict was not difficult to guess.

And in all this, none bothered to listen to Kadambari. They all had pre-formatted opinions. No one was willing to even think about the unborn child. It was clear she had become a liability for the royal family. They pressurized her for an abortion, but she remained adamantly supportive of her unborn child and decided to move to London, where she had an estate bestowed by her late mother. Nikki was all that she had now.

Kavya was born a few months later in London in 1993.

VIII

Shyam Pradosh had driven, rather fled from Angira in Kadambari's BMW that night along with her jewellery and cash. It had been nine years now, and he had invested his time and money productively in the real estate business. He changed cities frequently, but Nabinagar caught his attention. At that time, there were rumours about a new Airport coming up at Nabinagar. SP started buying land in that area. He was on a buying spree, but the rate he offered to the landowners, was a pittance.

One of the landowners, RK, refused the offer and had to pay with his life. His son, too, was grievously injured in the shootout. Fearing for their lives, the rest of the land owners meekly submitted to SP's demand. They had virtually no option, as SP's henchmen were dangerously inhuman. Lands were purchased in dummy names so that no direct connection could be pointed at him.

It was on Purnima that the official notification for Nabinagar Airport was announced. The day was super special, his daughter Mugdha's tenth birthday. She was her lucky charm and the light of his life. The full moon seemed to illuminate SP's fortune. Little did he care that he had inflicted darkness upon Kadambari, the same very ill-fated night nine years ago.

The official announcement of the Airport set the cash bells ringing for the realty sector, and it brought many new players to Nabinagar. It was a minuscule project as compared to other deals of Srikant Kali, but "small is beautiful", he said. As an astute businessman with ethics and values, he had created his empire brick by brick. Waiting for things to happen was not his cup of tea. He believed in working hard to make things happen. After all, Kali Industries was not built in a day.

Being a devout religious karma yogi, Kali Babu practised the scriptures in daily life. He read them every day and followed its words in letter and spirit. As a compassionate employer with a heart of gold, he led a simple life but ensured a comfortable life for his employees and their families.

Perhaps it was destined that the twain shall meet, as Kali Babu was invited as a speaker at an event in Nabinagar where SP happened to be the anchor. SP's oratory skills and ability to grasp new ideas drew immediate attention of Kali Babu.

SP was initially offered a consultant's job by Kali Babu, but his supply chain suggestions and localised business models soon boosted the company's revenues, and he gradually rose in the hierarchy. His tech-savvy, meticulous mind soon became an asset for Kali Babu's company.

Having gained the trust of the management, he now started offering his lands for sale at high rates. Since there were fictitious names, it was not easy to trace back the ownership to him. SP was not an economist but knew well that land was the scarcest factor of production. The buyers could be easily coerced to pay a premium for a land of their choice.

Suyash, the Finance manager at Kali Industries, approached him for help in getting the land deals done. Soon, it was good news as the first land sale was clinched. Then another, and soon the numbers grew. The company revenues were rising just as his good luck, and everything seemed to be going as per plan. SP's performance delighted Kali Babu, and he was asked to take the additional charge of finance as Suyash was going on leave. It was Suyash's marriage, and as per company rules, he was allowed a month's leave.

Kali Babu had thrown a lavish party for Suyash and his fiancée Suchita in the evening. The couple looked so beautiful together in twinning blue dresses. It was a great party with splendid arrangements, but the icing on the cake was Suchita's splendid rendition of an old classical song. Her voice was soothingly divine, and soon Suyash joined her. The way they looked into each other's eyes and held hands passionately while singing, the two seemed head over heels in love.

Kali Babu was known to be a principled man amongst his friends and foes alike, although it was difficult to say whether he had more friends than enemies. But one thing was certain: none could doubt his intentions and integrity. Hence, when the Nabinagar Airport Project went to Kali Industries, there was a sense of relief amongst the ruling elite, too.

The term of Vidhan Sabha was going to end soon, and in the ensuing election campaigns, any sort of corruption or underhand deals could have adversely affected the ruling dispensation. Chief Minister Sitara Devi and her National Party were running for their third consecutive term. Their victory was more or less certain as the main opposition party was a divided house, and its various factions were busy fighting amongst themselves.

It was the arrival of Mamak Vragji, the firebrand student leader, that rattled the ruling party. He came from a modest background and was immensely proud of it. He was young, eloquent and, most importantly, had no baggage of scams or corruption against him. For the last seven years since the formation of JSP, he was actively working at the ground level. This was the first time his party was contesting the elections. He connected easily with the masses as local issues formed the mainstay of his speeches.

Some of the issues appeared a bit intangible to be made an electoral plank, yet none of them were abstract to be overlooked. He knew the people's pulse and exhorted them to work together for problem resolution. His slogan, 'local problem, local solution', became a big hit with the masses.

His rallies had crowds pouring in, whereas other parties had to rely on crowd pullers like movie stars. Power to the people was not just a slogan for him; it was his earnest desire that the ordinary man should feel the power in his own hands. His strategy was trifold: *Jan Sahbhagita, shram daan and Bhrashtachar se mukti* [28]. His youth appeal had a massive fan following amongst youngsters, which helped his party spread its wings across the state.

One night, Mamak was returning home from the party office. His mind was preoccupied with the problem of negligible funds in the party account. How could his seven-year-old party fight elections on such a shoestring budget? He was hoping for some miracle, some permutation or combination

---

[28] *People's Participation, Voluntary Contribution of Labour and Freedom from Corruption*

that would lead him to the much-needed funds for electioneering.

But he wanted the donations to be hundred per cent transparent as well as ethical, and that is why Kali Babu was his best option. "But why would he fund a novice politician like me?" thought Mamak.

The clock tower near his house struck twelve, and the sound of bells broke his chain of thoughts. "I am Home!" He said aloud.

Just then, a car came out of nowhere. Mamak ducked to the right side of the road and fell into a pit as the car whizzed past him. It was a new car; even the number plates were not there. "Who the hell was he," thought Mamak, "driving at breakneck speed at this hour?"

Mamak was trying to come out of the pit when he heard the crashing sound. He brushed the mud on his clothes and ran towards the direction of the sound. The speeding car seemed to have hit the divider first and flipped in the air before hitting the ground on the other side of the road.

There was a person on the wheel, and Mamak heaved a sigh of relief when he saw that the steering wheel had spared his abdomen by a whisker of an inch. Mamak tried pulling him out, but the door didn't budge. It seemed to be jammed due to the impact of the collision. The man in the car looked unconscious; perhaps his left leg was entangled in the seat belt.

Mamak tried hitting the window glass, but nothing happened. So he began pulling all the gates one by one. The rear door opened with a jerk and Mamak stepped in to release the seat belt. His left leg was free now.

He carried the person to his home and called the local compounder for first aid. "Thankfully, there aren't major injuries; he should be alright by tomorrow morning, said the compounder. By the way, he is drunk. Had the police reached before you, he would have been in jail."

This was the first meeting of Mamak & SP. It was accidental literally, but it proved to be the foundation of their long-term association. SP needed political clout and backing, whereas Mamak was looking for money power to achieve political power. It was difficult to say who raised the first hand for friendship, Mamak or SP? But the seeds of their partnership were sown that night for sure.

The election schedule was announced next month. It was to be a single-phase election. Mamak was busy in his campaigns. The poll surveys were predicting a hung assembly with no political party getting a clear-cut majority. The political pundits were busy discussing post-poll alliance possibilities. Mamak was not ready for a coalition government, as that could hamper the implementation of his manifesto. "You worry too much," said SP, "If your Jan Sampark Party does not get a majority, I will arrange funds for horse trading."

"No," Mamak stomped his foot on the ground, "that's not my style of working. I stand for clean politics and would prefer to sit in opposition if I don't have the requisite numbers rather than join you in unethical action."

It was the last week for filing nominations. In politics, it is often said that a week is a long time. And the morning news changed everything. A huge quantity of highly pure bsowoxerin drug (valued at a hundred million dollars in the international market) had been found during the midnight raid at the farmhouse of Chief Minister Sitara Devi. And to add to her woes, the blood samples of her son Robin and his friends, who were partying at the farmhouse at the time of the raid, tested positive for bsowoxerin.

This huge quantity of drugs had been delivered by international peddlers at the farmhouse. Actually, it was a transit point for delivering it to various parts of the country. In spite of the heavy police deployment during electioneering, they took this risk under the impression that none would dare to check CM's farmhouse.

The first newspaper to run this breaking news was 'Janta Ka Sewak', and soon every newspaper jumped on the bandwagon. Suddenly, from oblivion, this small-time newspaper saw a surge in its sales. Very few people even knew CM's son's name before this incident. But now Robin was everywhere. Old photographs were being taken out, and character assassination was in full swing. In this media trial, none bothered to check whether any investigations had even begun ? The news was selling like hot cake, so who had time to check the details?

The media was rife with the CM's inability to instil good values in her son. Her ten years of governance were no more on the rating metre of the electorate. Personal life took precedence over professional life. The public perception about her changed overnight. One incident, and she was on the radar of critics. Her personal life was being washed in public as dirty linen. Her old speeches were taken out, and things she had said contextually were being quoted out of context and blown out of proportion. She was now seen as an elitist, status quo-perpetuating oligarch who fancied herself as an owner rather than a temporary holder of power.

"I think our opponents are behind this.Believe me, my son is in no way connected to this drug deal. He is being framed." Sitara Devi tried to plead before the party's high command, but it was of no use.""The party is above the individual," she was told tersely. The release of her resignation letter was the first step of damage control undertaken by the party. In short, the farmhouse raids ensured that Sitara Devi was shunted out of politics,at least for now. And it was a big relief for …

Sitara Devi's fall from grace was orchestrated by an old wily fox. Someone, even she had forgotten.

Has one ever seen a shadow in darkness?

IX

Campaigning was in full swing when SP dialled the Janta ka Sewak newspaper's editor, Babil. "Your newspaper sales seem to have risen in the last couple of days. Hope you have not forgotten my favour, which got you the fastest access to the news on CM's farmhouse raid. Won't you like to grow your readership numbers and foray into other states, too?"

"But we are a small newspaper, Sir. How are we going to compete with the revenue sharks?" Murmured Babil in a weak voice, knowing well that SP had called him on purpose and would never take 'no' for an answer.

"See, I will take care of your financial issues, but you have to act as the PR[29] manager of Mamak, albeit anonymously. I know he has a good follower base in the state, but it needs to be taken to the national level. Every day, there has to be some coverage, some positive narrative about his activities and interactions with the people. Of course, negative stories about his rivals could be of help, too. My legal team will be in touch with you for the formalities," said SP in a blunt tone and disconnected the phone.

The drug scandal had rocked the ruling National Party's boat, and their third consecutive term did not seem feasible anymore. The high command was worried as it was not just

---

[29] *Public Relations*

any state election but a very important one. It had the largest reserves of minerals in the country and was the only state with a surplus budget. They needed to retain power in the state at all costs. The party's poll machinery was swung into action to salvage its brand image.

SP kept tabs on the situation and patiently waited for the time when the National Party would be forced to come knocking at Mamak's door. He knew this was the do-or-die moment to gain a meaningful foothold in state politics. His game plan was to raise the initial stakes so that maximum flesh could be extracted at the negotiating table.

Meanwhile, the National Party campaign had now shifted gears, showing their Ex-Chief Minister as a victim of circumstances. Her hardships as a single mother whose son, unfortunately, fell in bad company were being highlighted across print and visual media. The party tried to brush it off as a one-time thing and put the blame squarely on Robin's friends. It was a last-ditch effort to garner a sympathy vote and tilt the scales in the National Party's favour.

Kamtej, the darling of media headlines, could be of help, mused SP. The son of royal scion Shakti Shubhankar, who abdicated the throne a few years ago, had made a mark in the legal fraternity as a firebrand lawyer. His championing of social causes often stirred up storms both inside and outside the courtrooms.

In Robinhood style, his nascent firm Victor Associates charged heavily from affluent clients but fought cases for the poor people, free of cost. The name of the firm underlined his attachment to his late friend Victor, who could have been saved on that fateful day had the rescue team considered all the children as equals. He shouted for help, but none heeded to his cries. Poor Victor did not stand a chance against the rich kids, whose survival was deemed more important.

In normal circumstances, it would have been difficult to convince apolitical Kamtej to take up this case due to its political overtones. But SP's task was made easy as CM's son Robin, too, had a friend named Victor who was taken away by the police during the raid on the farmhouse, and there was no news about his whereabouts since then. SP's team met Victor's family and discussed the case. Its various aspects were analysed, and the team suggested Victor's father, to approach Kamtej for legal help.

How could Kamtej say no to Victor's plea? This name was too close to his heart. He instantaneously agreed to fight the legal battle of namesake Victor, the friend of the Chief Minister's son.

By the time the ruling National Party could get wind of this development, a Habeas Corpus petition had been filed in the Hon'ble Supreme Court on Victor's behalf, and a public brouhaha had erupted over missing Victor. It was now the case ,wherein Victor had been sacrificed to save the mighty and powerful Chief Minister's son. 'Save Victor' campaigns were launched across the nation by the Jan Sampark Party, and the crusader Mamak Vragji became the talk of the town.

A state election soon hogged the national headlines, and the deteriorating law and order grabbed the media's attention. Sparks ignited across the nation, and it looked like SP's plan had succeeded.

These agitations rattled the central leadership of the National Party as they were now being targeted with uncomfortable questions. The National Party needed to deploy the fire fighting measures swiftly lest the issue turned into a full-fledged people's movement.

SIT (Special Investigating Team) was formed the very next morning, and an FIR (First Information Report), too, was filed against Sitara Devi and her son Robin under non-bailable sections. No Chief Minister had three consecutive terms in the state, and the jinx remained unbroken.

Voting was just three days away, and the ruling party had its fingers crossed. Whether the last-ditch push had any effect on the electorate would be known soon. The voting percentage was almost five per cent more than in the last election, but the exit poll results were not looking favourable for the ruling National Party.

It forced them to press the panic button, and they called Mamak for negotiation. SP had already envisioned this possibility and had advised him to not go for any talks at the local level. Three hours later, Mamak received a call from the National Party President for a meeting in the national capital.

The National Party was confident that after their offer of Chief Minister's chair to Mamak, he would readily toe their line. They had assumed it to be his only demand. "The powerful chair of CM being offered on a platter sounds like a dream come true for any newcomer in politics. What else could he aspire to," thought the National Party President.

The meeting began in a congenial environment with the usual niceties. "In spite of being the senior and larger party, our offer is magnanimous. We are ready to make you the Chief Minister," said the National Party President, hoping that Mamak would agree instantly.

Instead, Mamak sat still and spoke in a calm tone, "We will not be a part of the Government but will support it from the outside. Here is our Common Minimum Programme. Any deviation from it, will result in the withdrawal of our support from the government. There has to be a monthly meeting between our senior party leaders and the Chief Minister. In the meeting, the performance of ministers will be reviewed by us. In case a minister's work is found unsatisfactory, he/she will have to be dropped."

A visibly shocked National Party president went through the Common Minimum Programme. It was nothing but the election manifesto of the Jan Sampark Party. Mamak looked relaxed and composed, just like the confident puppeteer of the puppet show. There was pin-drop silence in the room as the grand old party was facing the dilemma of consenting to the demand of their Chief Minister and his Cabinet of Ministers being puppets to a new entrant in politics. But what other option did they have?

"President Rule? Going for another election? But it needs a lot of resources.This election has cost us a lot, and it is almost impossible to arrange funds for another election campaign at a short notice." They all waited with bated breath for the results, hoping that exit polls would be proven wrong.

To the utter dismay of the National Party, election results were on predictable lines. National Party had won forty-three, the main opposition party thirty-two, and Mamak's party had fifty-seven seats. Independents and small parties had won ten seats in the one hundred forty-two-member assembly.

Mamak's party emerged as the single largest party, and no government could be formed in the state without his support. There was jubiliation amongst Mamak's supporters as they thronged the roads across cities and villages.Theoretically, National Party and the main opposition party could come together to form a government. But its likelihood was similar to the sun rising in the west.

Now Mamak held all the aces in his hand, and the National Party President had nothing to counter. Till a few months ago, Mamak was ridiculed as the new kid on the block by the ruling party, and today, the entire script has been rewritten, with the main lead itself being changed. Politics is truly the art of the impossible drawn by the freestyle brush of irony.

The National Party consented to Mamak's demand lest he change his mind. A clean-image Chief Minister was appointed, and the Council of Ministers were chosen on the basis of merit. Everything seemed to be in place and going as planned. At the swearing-in ceremony, the Chief Minister, along with senior party functionaries, rose to welcome Mamak. They all were jostling to seek his blessings. The National Party President too stood up to salute the rising sun. "Friendship or enmity in politics are variables, they can change. It is the commonality of interests that remains constant." Kingmaker Mamak had arrived in style.

"Time to get down to brass tacks," said Mamak in an authoritarian tone. This soon became his signature style…

SP was forced to skip the swearing-in ceremony as he had gone to Harekrishna Nagar for the Buildcon Conference. Actually, Lenkesh was the primary reason for him being at Harekrishna Nagar. The conference was just secondary, a sort of add-on. Lenkesh now held a senior position at NODO, and it was not that easy to meet him at the office.

One of SP's associates had given him the news that Lenkesh had bought a beach house at Harekrishna Nagar. SP jumped on this opportunity and decided to gatecrash his party. He was not sure if Lenkesh would recognise the young lad from Sumerukhed village. In their last meeting, SP could not thank him properly, but this time, no excuses, he reminded himself!

Had Lenkesh not been there, SP would have remained stuck at Sumerukhed for life. Although there were important deals waiting to be closed, his desire to meet Lenkesh overtook all those considerations. Suyash was on a month's leave, and hence, SP knew that there was ample time to complete the unfinished work.

As far as ethics or morality was concerned, they were mere words for him; rather, he treated them as obstructions on the road to success. Achievement of personal goals was of utmost importance; whether by hook or crook, he didn't care.

SP was pacing near the gate of Triveni when a tennis ball hit his head. His natural reflex made him duck, and the ball landed safely in his hands. He looked in the direction of the ball and saw a lanky boy with the bat on the terrace. "That was a good catch! Wait, I am coming down to take the ball," he said.

The young boy played cricket for his University, and it did

not take much time to form a common bond on the cricket pitch. "The only thing that I will miss after my graduation this year is going to be my cricket team," he said with a smile.

Soon, the discussion veered to last night's match between New Zealand and England. The talking point was, of course, William's brilliant catch and the half-century by Grayson. "Yes, the match was like a potboiler; it had beautiful shots, absolute yorkers and a comic run out, too, when both the batsmen were marooned on the same side of the wicket. It was a high five on that note. Hey, I am SP!"

"And I am Atrin, why don't you join us, come meet my parents. Actually, we are having a party in Triveni, our new house, as he held SP's hand at the gate. Papa, see my new friend," shouted Atrin. And there he was, smiling as always. Just a bit of grey hair and a French-cut beard; nothing else had changed.

SP stood still and fumbled with his thank you as Atrin introduced him to his father as SP (Super Player) of cricket. Lenkesh shook hands with him and moved on towards other guests. SP would have continued with his awe-struck posture had it not been for Atrin tugging at his arm, "Let's go and play cricket on the terrace."

By the time SP returned to the party with Atrin, Lenkesh had left. SP decided to wait for his time rather than hurrying the plan. Although he was a bit disappointed to miss the opportunity to have a one-on-one with Lenkesh today, at least he had gained a bonus - a gate pass called Atrin!

Lenkesh was not one of those media byte guys who came frequently on television. He was working on important ocean projects, and it was his work that garnered eyeballs. SP's sources told him that the current government was also supportive of his nascent programmes. However, research and exploration work have long gestation periods, and whether the support and finances would continue for a protracted time is an open, unanswered question as of now.

He came to know from his sources that Lenkesh was scouting for financiers for his capital-intensive ocean projects and SP thought of extending a helping hand to Lenkesh as his thank-you gesture. He intended to rope in politician Mamak in the game plan to forge an alliance in the long run. "The nexus between popular politician Mamak, genius scientist Lenkesh and shrewd businessman like me would be nothing short of a godsend gift. This troika could change the destinies of people one day," said SP.

SP had been a fervent cricket fan since his childhood, but his catching skills were reaping rich dividends for him now. A chance catch at Sarvesh Kalia Stadium, Roop Nagar, had led to lady luck smiling upon him. Years later, could this fortuitous catch encounter with Lenkesh's son at Triveni, Harekrishna Nagar, be a match-winner again?

"Catches win matches" is more than just a cliché. SP had his fingers crossed.

X

Kali Babu had thought of sending a junior executive for the Buildcon Conference; after all, it was just an annual exercise. But SP insisted that a senior functionary like him should go to explore the new business opportunities at Harekrishna Nagar as it was being held for the first time in a non-metro town. Kali Babu agreed although he had a hunch of it being a cock and bull story.

Of late, he had been getting reports about certain financial irregularities in new land deals and decided to use SP's absence to check the details. "The paperwork in the department seemed good enough, not needing any further scrutiny," thought Kali Babu. But he wanted to be doubly sure, so he accessed SP's computer remotely. There were several password-protected files in SP's personal folder. The names of the files were intriguing, like 2/66/17, 7/104/34, and 15/28/87. There were fifteen such files in the folder. Was it a mere coincidence that the number of files on the computer and the land deals finalised by SP matched?

What was the meaning of these numbers? Were they following any increasing or decreasing order? Kali Babu looked at the numbers carefully. Well, some did, and some did not. Adding up these numbers also did not make any sense, and neither did they seem to denote alphabets in Hindi or English. The numbers appeared random at the outset, but they could literally mean anything under the sun, mused Kali

Babu as he re-examined the numbers. But why had SP kept such complicated numbers as file names?

Tired of looking at the numbers repetitively, he closed his eyes for a few seconds. Stress is not good for you; he recalled his doctor's advice. Kali Babu's health had been deteriorating of late, but he preferred not to discuss this in public or with his employees. Only Suyash knew about it, as he used to accompany Kali Babu for check-ups.

He looked at the bottle of emergency pills in the drawer and exhaled slowly. "The doctor had strictly instructed me to take the pill in case of an emergency. But I don't think I am ever going to need them. After all, I am taking my daily medicines on time and following the doctor's advice in toto," said Kali Babu aloud.

"Maybe narrowing down his search criterion could be of help. Are the numbers pointing to some geographical coordinates, maybe the longitude and latitude written in a code? Okay, let me check in the library."

Being a voracious reader, he had set up a small library in the office premises itself. He encouraged his staff for the book reading sessions, and whenever Kali Babu could take some time out of his busy schedule, he would also join them.

The books were arranged in a very methodical way. He sat on his favourite hand-carved Sheesham wood rocking chair. The beautifully designed chair with premium embossed finishing had a regal look and a sense of weightlessness as he rocked to and fro! "Nothing has changed since my last visit," thought Kali Babu. There was pin-drop silence in the room, punctuated by the rocking sound of his chair.

Well, it could be a book. Kali Babu sprang from his chair. The first file was 2/66/17; he looked for book number 2, opened page number 66 and searched for word number 17. The word was Sidhi. He looked at the list of people from whom lands had been purchased recently, and right there on the top of the list, was Sidhi. He looked at the second file, 7/104/34. Was it book number 7, page number 104 and word number 34? Yes, Bindeshwar, the name matched again! And thereafter, it didn't take much time to get the list of the entire fifteen sellers' names.

"File names are secretive, fishy SP. Now let's see what you have used as a password," Kali Babu said aloud. Each file was password-protected. One common thing in all the passwords was their length. They all had ten characters. He started writing the options. Could it be the date of birth? Nope, it had only eight characters. Then, was it a combination of name and year of birth? The probabilities sounded endless. "This hit-and-trial approach would take a long time. Should I call the system engineer to crack this password?" Thought Kali Babu.

"But what if SP is not guilty? I am yet to find his direct link to this fraud. Okay, let me try the password analyser, the in-house tool made by the IT team." As Kali Babu initiated the program on his desktop, he crossed his fingers, hoping that the passwords were not stored as a hash function.

Just then, the landline rang. It was one of his business associates cum close friend, J.Satya, on the line. "Ah, I know tomorrow is your 25th marriage anniversary. Best wishes, Satya. How are the preparations going? I will be at your home, Sunday at eight pm," said Kali Babu, trying to cut short the conversation as courteously as he could. Had it been another day, this call could have easily lasted an hour!

The landline was to the right of the table, and his desktop was facing the window on the opposite side. He rushed towards the desktop to see the results of the password analyser as soon as he put the receiver down.

"Thank God! It is a plain text and is a combination of capital letters and numbers with no special characters. The first five characters are alphabets followed by four numerals, and the last character is again an alphabet."

He took a deep breath and tapped the index finger on his lips. One look at the Excel sheet of the seller's details, and he started smiling. Confidently, he tapped at the file of Sidhi (2/66/17) and keyed in the password, and the file opened. Yes, he had guessed it right! It was the PAN number of the seller.

For a second, Kali Babu was overjoyed to have cracked the code."Sherlock Holmes would have been proud of me today," the child in him prompted to pat his own back. He did the customary three claps as he used to do in childhood.

But all this happiness disappeared in thin air, and his face turned crimson when he went through the fifteen files. He had never before seen such bungling in the office records. There were two sets of documents, identical in most parameters but differed where it mattered the most.

The land sale fraud was a part of a big conspiracy. The revenues were being looted in a cloak-and-dagger operation. It was then that Kali Babu dialled his most trusted lieutenant, Suyash and asked him to come home.

"It must be something important," wondered Suyash; otherwise, "Kali Sir would not have asked me to cut short my marriage leave and come ASAP and that too on a Saturday. But why has he called me at home rather than the office? I hope he is okay."

"I will be back soon," he told his family as he booked a cab. "Your marriage preparations are underway, how can you go," said his Uncle angrily, "There is so much work to be done, and Suchita's family is also coming from Chandinagar. What will we tell them about your absence?"

"Just say I am with Kali Babu." His family's anger subsided the moment they heard Kali Babu's name. They all knew how much he loved Suyash. "Please convey our best wishes and request him to join us at least a day before marriage. He is like our family member," said his Uncle.

"Maybe SP has gone to attend the Buildcon conference at Harekrishna Nagar, and some pressing matter has cropped up," thought Suyash as the cab moved towards the main road of Nabinagar. His ancestral house was in the old town, and Kali Babu lived in New Town. It normally took forty-five minutes, but sudden rain and storm had caused traffic mayhem, which delayed his arrival at Kali Babu's house.

He knocked gently and waited for a few seconds before entering the study room. What the hell had happened to the tidy and orderly room? Had he entered the wrong room, or had some hurricane just passed through?

Papers were scattered all across the room. Kali Babu's voice trembled with disbelief and denial as he asked Suyash to go through the papers. It was not a case of mismatch in minor heads, but there were manipulations in the entire balance sheet. Now he knew why SP had taken so much trouble to protect his personal folder.

Overstated revenues, false invoices, misstated financial conditions, it's a complete mess. "Just look at this. The Company's account is being debited for land deals, but the money is being credited to a single overseas account. This two plus two does not make four," said bewildered Kali Babu, looking at Suyash. He carefully went through all the papers again and hung his head. "Sir, it is a perfect fraud, not visible to the naked eye."

Kali Babu looked up. He had used the same phrase recently when one of his close friend's companies was sabotaged by an insider. Through falsification of documents and misappropriations, his friend's company had been crippled by the fraudster.

"SP was the first person to whom I told this," said Kali Babu as he banged his fist on the table. "I thought he was new to the corporate world and hence discussed it threadbare, explaining how the fraudsters manage to override the red flags in the system. I told him to check our systems for any loopholes of this kind, and he duped me only. I made myself a sitting duck."

There was another bunch of papers on the table which had SP's Swiss bank account numbers and details of shell companies in the Cayman Islands and various other places. "Oh My God, SP was plundering the company's money for filling his own kitty!" Kali looked at the hourglass on his table. "Just like this hourglass, sand was dropping from our company to SP's vaults." Suyash went through the account details once again and returned the papers to Kali Babu, who looked crestfallen beyond words.

There was a moment of silence in the room. Then Kali Babu regained his composure and said, "I will handle this myself. Don't speak to anyone about this till Monday morning. I found these papers in the office just before I called you. Let them be here at my home till I speak to SP.

Just imagine, all this was happening in my office, under my nose! And all this evidence was right there in my office!" He was pacing in the room, perhaps planning his next step. "You go home now," said Kali Babu, "A yellow alert has been issued by the meteorological department. Just look outside; the rainstorm rumblings are pounding against the windows!"

"Wait, I will tell my driver to drop you home." That's Kali Babu, always treating his employees as family.

The driver was waiting outside, but the water level in the street had started rising. "I think we should wait for some time as it does not seem safe to drive now," said Suyash. "There is a café on the other side of the road. I will wait there. You drop me home once the water recedes."

"Sir, why don't you stay here with Kali Babu till the rain stops?" "No, I will be at the café as I have to finish some work." Suyash knew that Saturday afternoon was meditation time for Kali Babu. A pious Hindu by Karmana, Manasa and Vachana [30], he was a true practitioner of the Bhagavad Gita.

---

[30] *deed, thought and word*

How could SP backstab such a noble person?

Suyash ordered a latte cappuccino and grabbed a seat near the window. Inside the café, people were glued to the television screen as the recording of the Wimbledon Men's Tennis match between Pete Sampras and Roger Federer was being telecast.

But he was not in the mood today to watch the match. There was a drawing board near his coffee table where people could post their drawings. He took a sheet and a pencil and closed his eyes.

It was after a long time that he was testing his eidetic (photographic) memory. The account numbers, names, addresses, he started scribbling them all. By the time he finished his coffee, the list was complete. As the waiter came with the bill, he was tucking the paper safely back into his pocket. "Why don't you put it on the board?" The waiter asked with a smile. "Ah, it's not yet complete," Suyash grinned back. By now, the rains had subdued, and the water level on the streets was beginning to recede.

"Maybe the Mayor has got the sump houses working at last," commented the person sitting next to Suyash. Smiling wryly, Suyash moved towards the café's exit.

It was then he saw a young boy standing on the pavement outside the cafe with a bunch of unsold newspapers on his bicycle. Suyash stood for a while and then asked the boy for a newspaper. "Sir, I don't have a national edition, as the rains have disrupted today's supply. But I have the local edition," he said in a sombre tone.

"Okay, how many papers do you have?" Asked Suyash. "I have fifty, but why are you asking?" This time, his tone was a bit aggressive. "Oh, that's great! Give me all," said Suyash, taking out his wallet.

"But are you going to read fifty newspapers?" He asked indignantly. It was clear the young lad was not in the mood to receive charity. "Oh no, these newspapers are not for me. It is for an institution," replied Suyash.

The young boy had seen the driver waiting for Suyash and shot back an angry glance. "Ah, don't be mistaken. That is my boss's car, not mine and here are your fifty rupees." "Wait, sir, fifty newspapers, if bought in a lot, entail a discount of three rupees. And there you go," he said, handing three one-rupee coins to Suyash.

Honesty in poverty is a virtue. Suyash's eyes were getting misty as he tried in vain to control his tears. "Sir, I am Diganta," the boy introduced himself politely. "One day, I want to be a Police Officer."

"Yes, you will surely achieve your dream," said Suyash, caressing his curly hair. The dimpled smile on Diganta's face seemed to light up the overcast sky. He waved his hands as Suyash's car sped away. The driver was amused to see the fifty newspapers.

"Sir, what are you going to do with so many newspapers? By the way, I know this boy. His mother, Kammo, is suffering from some serious disease and is admitted to the City hospital," said the driver.

"Oh, that is so sad! But wait, I know one senior doctor, Bijoy, in that hospital. You drop me at the hospital gate, my flat is nearby only," said Suyash. But Sir, I thought you would be going to your parents' house in the old town.

"Nah! I have some work here at home," said Suyash.

"And yes, don't forget to give these newspapers to the government-run hostel near the clock tower. Many students stay there for competitive exams."

"That is a good idea, Sir," said the driver as he stopped the car at the main gate of City Hospital.

Suyash alighted from the car and moved towards the doctor's chamber. "It's good to see you," said Dr Bijoy, hugging Suyash. "So what brings my old friend here? It must be some specific purpose; otherwise, your life revolves around Kali Babu only."

Suyash's friends knew that Kali Babu was like a father figure to him. They often pulled his leg for devotion and attachment towards his boss.

"It's about your patient Kammo," said Suyash. "Oh! She is suffering from Multiple Myeloma, a type of blood cancer. She is on chemotherapy right now, but if her condition doesn't improve, she might need a bone marrow transplant. The treatment is quite costly, and her chances of survival are very slim. But how are you related to her?" Asked Bijoy.

"I just now met her son Diganta," said Suyash, "You have to save her, Bijoy. I know this is a small hospital. If need be, please arrange to send her to the Super Speciality Cancer Hospital at Charbania. Don't worry about the costs; I will pay her bills."

Suyash immediately took out his chequebook and, thrust a blank signed cheque in Dr Bijoy's hand and headed outside, waving goodbye. "Wait, the tea is coming, said Bijoy." "Let's have it some other day," replied Suyash. I am hard-pressed for time today.

As he came out of the hospital, intermittent rain had started again. Had it been any other day, he would have enjoyed the tiny droplets falling on his face. But today, he was too angry with himself for failing to see through the fraudulent land deals.

As he entered his flat, there were two images of the day. One of innocent Diganta, and the other of cunning fraudster SP. He was deeply impressed with Diganta's vision of life. But it was the second image that escalated his anger.

"Someone just pops out of nowhere and bamboozles the company! I just can't let this happen," avowed Suyash.

XI

It was a misty Sunday morning at Nabinagar when SP decided to go to Kali Babu's house with sweet packets of 'Kaju Katli[31]' and 'Motichoor ke Laddoo'[32]. He was well aware of the sweet tooth of Kali Babu. He parked his car in the back lane as the front road had been closed for repairs from six in the morning till six in the evening. Kali Babu's house was about five minutes walk from there.

The house was surrounded by an alluring mix of flowers and fragrances in the garden. The wind chimes of various shapes and sizes, with its gentle tinkling to the noisy clanging, seemed to create an interesting melody. The garden was blessed with the hues of artistic dreams, soft yet bold pastels emboldening its rustic charm.

As he approached the house, the back door was slightly ajar. Kali Babu had told him once that every Sunday, most of the helpers have a weekly off. The gardener Garibdas, who lived nearby, often left the back door open. He would come and water the plants in the evening as Kali Babu was very much attached to the garden and called his masterpiece landscape 'a perfect blend of order and chaos'.

---

[31] *A diamond-shaped sweet decorated with edible silver coating. It is made with cashew nuts, sugar, cardamom powder, and condensed milk.*

[32] *Motichur laddu are soft, delish melt-in-the-mouth sweet balls made mainly with gram flour, sugar, and spices. It is a popular sweet from North Indian cuisine and is often made during festivals or celebrations.*

This was the first time SP was using the back door of the house. He was a bit uncertain as he slightly pushed the door open and entered the gardener's room. There was an alley leading to the main house. At the end of the alley, there was a locked door. "How stupid of me! Why would anyone keep the door open?" SP spoke aloud as he turned his back and moved towards the rear door.

"Garibdas, have you come back early today?" It was Kali Babu's voice from the other side of the door.

"No, Sir, it is me, SP, with your favourite sweets." Kali Babu opened the door and let him in. SP offered him the sweets, but he declined and continued to move towards his study room, signalling SP to follow.

"A lot has happened here in your absence. Come, I need to show you something," said Kali Babu as they entered the study. "By the way, how was your Conference at Harekrishna Nagar?"

SP was taken aback by this sudden change in Kali Babu's demeanour. Saying no to sweets was a bit unusual. "Ah, the Conference was great!" SP replied politely. "The place is developing fast, and there are ample business opportunities. I think we should set up our new office at Harekrishna Nagar. I have seen a good site at a very reasonable price. The owner is willing to negotiate also," said SP.

Kali Babu's face was livid with anger as he settled in his chair. He looked straight into SP's eyes and asked, "First, tell me, how many deals have you closed in Suyash's absence?" "Sir, I have closed fifteen deals, and the rest will be closed before Suyash returns from leave. He is getting married this week, and we should not be burdening him with so much work," chuckled SP, totally unaware of the storm that was about to arrive.

"Suyash has joined the office."

Kali Babu's words struck SP like lightning. His face turned white as he tried to regain composure. SP had not at all expected this. "Suyash came early," he fumbled, "but why?"

"I called him!" Shouted Kali Babu as he threw the land deal papers on SP's face.

"Sir, let me explain," pleaded SP, "It is not what you are thinking. I know many people at Nabinagar and was just using my network to help the company."

"No, you were trying to help yourself at the cost of the company," yelled Kali Babu as his eyes blazed with fierce indignation. "You have brought a bad name to my company and tarnished my image. You are nothing but a parasite feeding on the success of my company. How dare you use my company as a ladder for your ulterior motives?" Asked Kali Babu, fuming with anger.

"I am going to press charges against you on Monday. But before that, I am giving you twenty-four hours to make up our losses and surrender to the police." Kali Babu's body was shaking and sweating profusely as he called SP a fraud."I don't know how you manage to sleep at night? You are nothing but a harbinger of darkness,who sold his conscience to the devil."

Kali Babu was feeling uneasy as his heart was beating rapidly. He paused for a moment to catch his breath.Then he pulled the drawer and took out his bottle of emergency pills. With wobbling hands, he tried opening its cap. But the bottle seemed to be tightly shut, and as he tried to apply pressure, the bottle slipped from his hand and fell to the ground.

The pills scattered on the floor as he watched helplessly. He tried picking up the glass of water on the table, but his body fell to the ground with his outstretched hand still struggling to reach the pills.

"Please help me, Kali Babu moaned in a quivering voice. I am not able to breathe. Call my family doctor immediately. My vision, too, is blurring. I need those medicines urgently."

But SP stood still, like a statue. He seemed totally unconcerned with the pain and suffering of Kali Babu. "You were creating obstruction between me and Kali Industries.My young blood can take this company to greater heights.Your time is up."

Kali Babu was trying to pull the landline down when SP stepped forward and disconnected its wire with a wicked smile.Then he sat on Kali Babu's chair and closed his eyes for a moment. "Ah,it is feeling so good.I didn't know that power lies not in a person but in the chair!"

He was now alone in the room as Kali Babu's breathing sounds grew fainter .

After waiting for a while, SP picked up the land deal files from the table and moved towards the door. Then he turned back menacingly and collected all the pills, put them back in the bottle and kept it neatly in the drawer.He rearranged the room,reconnected the phone and kept everything at its place, as if nothing had happened.

He cast a quick look at Kali Babu, who was lying still with eyes staring at the ceiling. SP cleaned his fingerprints and left discreetly from the backdoor, along with all the papers.

He had time till tomorrow morning to make up a foolproof story. "By the way, what is the need," thought SP, as no one had seen him either enter or leave Kali Babu's house.

"But I need to close all the deals today itself, leaving nothing to chance." His mind was working on a new plan. Reaching the top was his goal, and the opportunity was knocking at his door. Now, Kali Industries needed a new owner, and of course, he suited the bill completely. He needed to play the emotional card at the right time to bring the board members to his side so that they treated him as the real heir of Kali Industries.

"Kali Babu, a bachelor by choice treated the staff members as his family. So, one of us should rightfully be his successor! Show time for the 'actor SP'," he said, looking at the mirror.

Since he left Angira, he didn't get much opportunity to showcase his acting skills. But now he had to convince the world how deeply he had been hurt by Kali Babu's demise. His flowing tears would bear testimony to his being Kali Babu's favourite employee. For someone like SP, who didn't shed a single tear at his own father's death, grieving for Kali Babu was going to be a perfect test of his acting skills. By evening, with all deals under his belt, SP's reign had begun.

Meanwhile marriage anniversary celebrations at J.Satya's house were in full swing. Most of the guests had arrived, but his eyes were looking for Kali Babu. He was not only his business associate but a very dear friend. "He had promised to reach by eight p.m., but now it is thirty minutes past eight," said J.Satya anxiously looking at his watch.

"Maybe he is stuck in the traffic," remarked one of the guests. J.Satya knew that his friend could never be late. He was so punctual that one could set the clock's time as per his itinerary. If he said eight, it could not be even five minutes past eight. Something seemed just not right to J.Satya!

It was nine p.m. now, but still no signs of him. J.Satya was getting restless and decided to go to Kali Babu's house to check on him. "I will be back in half an hour. Take care of the guests in my absence," he told his daughter.

Kali Babu's house was pitch-dark. "So unusual," said J.Satya as he rang the bell. There was no response. Then he knocked on the door loudly. Hearing the commotion, Kali Babu's neighbour, Keyur, came out hurriedly. "What's the matter? Why is Kali Babu not opening the door?" J.Satya asked him. "Has he gone somewhere?"

"No, I didn't see him leave. The road repair work was slated for today, so the whole day we were indoors only. And on Sundays, generally, his house helps have the weekly off. Only the cook comes back by evening. But yesterday, I overheard Kali Babu telling the cook not to come as he had a dinner invitation," said Keyur.

"Let's try the back door. It might be open." Both of them went to the gardener's room. Garibdas was not there, so they pushed the door into the alley. It opened with a creaking sound. J.Satya switched on the lights and looked around. The house seemed to be in order. Both of them started calling Kali Babu, but the house remained silent as before.

As they opened the door of the study, J.Satya rushed to his friend lying on the floor and attempted CPR (Cardio Pulmonary Resuscitation). But it was too late. Keyur's wails brought his family and other neighbours to Kali Babu's house. Soon, the police arrived on the scene. They suspected foul play as the back door was open and registered a case of unnatural death. The news spread like wildfire.

SP had played his cards well and was sure that Kali Babu's demise would not be noticed till Monday morning. But he was now caught on the wrong foot. Not that he felt any remorse or pangs of guilt for not helping Kali Babu in his last moments; rather, he immediately jumped on it as an opportunity.

Actually, he was one of those guys who wallowed in their own sense of victimhood and bore a grudge against society rather than using their pains as part of their emotional transformation toward an empathic self.

It was his sheer luck that the investigating officer appointed in this case was ASI Siraj, who happened to be a big fan of Mamak. SP had met him often, monitoring the law and order at Mamak's rallies. This eased SP's pressure of keeping tabs on the investigations.

The demise of Kali Babu devastated Suyash. He looked for the bottle of emergency pills in the drawer; they were intact.

"Why didn't he take the pills if he was unwell? The room was absolutely in order when his body was discovered by J.Satya and Keyur. Who had set the room in order after I left on Saturday? Where are the original files?

There is definitely a strong possibility of someone being in the room at the time of his death. Police need to expeditiously trace the man who last saw Kali Babu alive. I must tell them about my meeting with Kali Babu."

ASI Siraj was not at the police station, so Suyash left a message for him. The prayer meeting at his home was to begin in about half an hour. Suyash needed to pay his final respects to Kali Babu who treated him like his own son, "Our beautiful relationship will stay with me forever. You are going to live in my heart till my last breath," said Suyash as he wiped his tears.

SP had observed a change in the body language of Suyash since his return from Harekrishna Nagar. "Why is he avoiding me? Maybe he is traumatised by the sudden demise of boss," thought SP, "I will speak to him after the prayer meeting."

Then, he saw the investigating officer entering the prayer hall. "Hey Siraj, have you come for the prayer meet?" Asked SP. Siraj nodded his head. "Kali Babu was a nobleman. May his soul rest in peace! By the way, who is Suyash? He had come to the police station with some information regarding this case."

Suyash, who was on the other side of the prayer hall, saw SP pointing towards him while talking with Siraj. He could sense the unease on ASI Siraj's face. SP was definitely saying something against him as both looked in his direction. He needed to guard the envelope of proof in his hand from fraudster SP. The evidence had to be protected at all costs.

Then he saw Diganta with the flower tray. Seizing the opportunity, he handed over the envelope to Diganta. "Keep it safely with you," he said in a hushed voice. "Leave this place immediately. And in case someone asks you, we never met, and this conversation never happened."

Hardships of life had thrust maturity on Diganta at an early age. His mother's life-threatening disease had shaken Diganta, and he had almost lost hope. But it was the saviour, Suyash who came out of nowhere and fulfilled her wish of good health.

Come what may, he was bound to stand up for his good samaritan. Diganta slid the envelope beneath the flower tray, and acting as the flower supplier guy, mingled in the crowd and took an exit towards the flower truck. Handing over the empty tray to the driver, he disappeared in the by-lanes.

To divert attention from him, SP knew that he needed one name. Someone who had the motive as well as the opportunity to kill Kali Babu, would fit the bill. Initially, he did not want to implicate Suyash as they had become good friends, but his ethical activism left SP with no choice. He was not sure of the evidence in Suyash's possession but had a hunch that it was going to be music to the police's ears. He needed to make the first move swiftly to take advantage against Suyash and discredit whatever proof he had.

He told ASI Siraj that Kali Babu suspected Suyash of making falsified entries in the balance sheet. That is why he was recalled from leave. Kali Babu had confronted him with documentary proof and warned of action being initiated against him, said SP. He was asked to sign a confession letter.

"The driver also told me that Suyash was the last person from our staff side to meet Kali Babu," he added.

Suyash was summoned by police for questioning. He tried to explain, but ASI Siraj's mind had already accepted him as guilty. Suyash was not given a fair chance. Planted stories in friendly newspapers like the 'Janta ka Sewak' made Suyash appear like a leech sucking his master's blood. 'Gentleman Suyash' was no match for 'swindler SP's' manipulative moves.

Kali Babu was hugely popular in the state. His death sent shockwaves through the community. People came out in the streets demanding swift action against the guilty, which made SP's task easier. Suyash was vilified as a serial offender. The bliss and gaiety of his marriage preparations were marred as the public pronounced him guilty and directed its anger on his family.

His character assassination humiliated the family so much that they severed all relations with him. Even Suchita's family was not spared, and they suffered personal ignominy in society. Her family cancelled the marriage, yet the finger-pointing and mudslinging did not abate. Mortified by public disgrace, Suchita left her family at Chandinagar and never came back.

The case was tried in a fast-track court. SP got witnesses who testified against Suyash and ensured that the circumstantial evidence was piled against him. Such was the public angst against Suyash that even his own lawyer wilfully turned slow on rebuttals and cross-questioning.

Blackstone's criminal law principle, 'better that ten guilty persons escape, than that one innocent suffer', was not adhered to. As the verdict was being pronounced, tears of helplessness flowed down his cheeks. People in the Courtroom thought that he was scared of going to prison. Soon innocent Suyash was sentenced for life (imprisonment for the balance of his natural life).

"How would the people in the Courtroom know that the judgement ruined the life of an innocent Suchita who had nothing to do with all this? She was made to pay the price for Suyash's righteousness. And the worst part was that the perpetrator of the ghastly crime against Kali Babu was still roaming free and was about to take over the Kali Industries."

Very soon, this prophecy came true. As the new owner of Kali Industries, SP donned a new avatar in which he chose magic over method and control over procedures. His new image was neither cautious nor collaborative. His network had grown stronger, and so had his money power. People joined him wilfully, or else he resorted to money tactics.

"One needs to know the right price and quote it at the right time," he often said. The story, which began in 1983 at Sumerukhed, had completed eighteen years as Shyam Pradosh arrived in style. The number eighteen implied that the age of being a minor was gone. He was no more the novice from Sumerukhed. SP turned pro at Nabinagar.

XII

It was the quadricentennial celebration at the National Oceanic Defence Organisation, Lalpura, and the year was 2004. The journey had begun twenty-five years ago in an abstract-looking building in a bye-lane surrounded by trees at Lalpura. Most of its employees at that time used to come by city bus and would get down at the Beadon Street stop. It was a two minutes' walk from there. Old residents of Lalpura still call it the Auditor's Office. The phone signals rarely worked in its vicinity. The jammers ensured minimal activities near the NODO building!

There was a buzz in the office as Senior Scientist Lenkesh was expected to unveil the findings of his ocean research project during the celebrations tonight. Many in the office believed that the announcement regarding his promotion was on the cards. Lenkesh, too, was confident about that as he looked proudly at pictures of Trinetra, the submersible on his personal laptop. It was the fructification of years of research and single-minded pursuit of his dreams.

The submersible could seamlessly move above the sea floor, surveying the seabed beneath. The spherical eyeball-shaped submersible was laced with built-in digital cameras and a multi-beam echo sounder. The powerful dual tool manipulators ensured easier movements, particularly when it wished to return to the ocean's wealth.

Lenkesh staunchly believed that the world's future lay in the deep ocean bed. But his problem lay in the fact that the requisite research and underwater missions needed huge funds, and yet the budgetary allocations for his department were getting squeezed year on year. He had been pleading for funding from the head office but to no avail. The doors were getting closed one by one, leaving him with very few options.

Had it not been for SP's financers in the last couple of years, his research work would have been stalled for sure. The latest angel investor introduced by SP offered to invest crores in his mission. Lenkesh was elated but, in his excitement, forgot that there are no free lunches…

Thanks to the generous funding by this new investor, Trinetra, as well as the futuristic lab with cutting-edge technologies, had become a reality in such a short period of time. It had everything he needed for his research and exploration missions. Although its docking station at Tarulia was in the investor's control, Lenkesh ensured that he had the operating codes.

But last month, the investors asked for Trinetra's codes. Now, that was too much; sharing the codes was out of the question. Lenkesh sat on the proposal for a week but had to relent at last. Then he put a precondition; he would be in the submersible every time it goes under water. Trinetra was his soul, and Lenkesh could never allow anyone else to operate it.

He had managed to keep Trinetra under wraps at NODO and had divulged only its initial prototype to the board members. Today, he was planning to showcase Trinetra at the foundation day ceremony. "Trinetra, the queen, is going to rock the show tonight," said Lenkesh proudly.

"The CEO would be too happy once I share these details with him, particularly the findings related to the exploration of non-active hydrothermal vents," thought Lenkesh, "These ocean vents (i.e. the fissures in the ocean floor spewing hot gases and liquids) had ceased venting, and further research could lead to new discoveries."

He was confident that the CEO would understand the reasons for keeping Trinetra at a private docking station at Tarulia. "Outcomes were more important, not the procedures," thought Lenkesh. All this research, making of Trinetra and subsequent underwater explorations, needed huge capital, and hence, he avoided wading into the ethical 'Means vs. Ends' debate. After all, history remembers only the winners!

The private phone rang in his cabin twice. He immediately picked up the CEO's phone. The red bulb outside his cabin flashed intermittently, signalling 'no entry'. There was jubilation in the office as the staff members thought that Lenkesh's promotion order had come. It was meant to be announced at the evening function, but it seems they have decided to go ahead with the good news. "Earlier, the better," remarked one of the staff.

A few of them were standing outside Lenkesh's cabin, waiting for him to step out. Almost ten minutes had elapsed, when Lenkesh's secretary came out trembling with trepidation. "CEO Sir has asked all the staff members to assemble in the hall," he said.

There were murmurs as they saw Lenkesh coming out of the chamber with his head and shoulders drooping in a sigh of resignation. "What happened to Sir?" Asked Surti. "Today is a special day for him and his crowning glory, Trinetra. But why is he so upset?" Said Sanya. The secretary signalled both of them to be silent.

Surprised by the sudden turn of events, the staff members followed him to the hall. "How dare you?" Shouted the CEO. His team members were aghast to see the gentle CEO yelling so loudly at Lenkesh.

"You offered the organisation on a platter to the private miners! You are a traitor, and I dismiss you instantly from this august organisation. A case has been initiated against you, and soon you will be behind bars." CEO's face was smouldering with rage.

"Dr Chandrasi would be replacing you," he said, pointing towards her. "Chandrasi, this promotion is not only for you but for the people you lead."

Then, looking disparagingly at Lenkesh, he continued, "My people at NODO deserve a better leader, not someone like you who sold his integrity to the devil for a few golden coins."

He turned towards Dr Chandrasi and asked her to join him on the Delta line in five minutes. "See you all at the foundation day celebrations tonight," said the CEO, waving his right hand. The staff members began exiting the hall in stunned silence. They all knew the importance of the Delta line, a secure communication used only in emergencies.

Lenkesh sank into the chair in the conference hall, holding his head in his hands. He had planned to showcase his research findings to the CEO today, on the foundation day. On the contrary, the CEO chose to disgrace him in front of his staff. Instead of patting his back, the CEO launched a bitter diatribe against him.

"After all, what was my mistake? I needed huge funds for this research, and the angel investor was ready to loosen the purse strings. In return, I had to relent to angel investors' private miners accompanying me in Trinetra. What other option did I have?"

Humiliated in his own office, in front of his own staff, it was too hard to bear. All his years of research, hard work and reputation were snatched in a second. And to add salt to his wounds, Chandrasi, his junior, was given his position. That, too, a female! How could she replace him? His face flushed with indignation as he recalled the berating treatment meted out to him by the CEO.

"How could he harangue like that? I gave all my life to this organisation, and this is what I get in return? I worked with utmost devotion on this project, and yet they kicked me out. They can dislodge and discredit the scientist Lenkesh from this project, but they cannot take away the ideas deeply rooted in my mind. NODO's main office in Lalpura is nothing without me."

Mad with fury, he rose from the chair and used the fire exit to bid adieu to the organisation which had been his purpose in life till a few minutes ago.

He knew that the internal security team would have entered his cabin by now. He was imagining their faces when nothing substantial would come up in their search. Lenkesh always worked with soft copies. Printouts were a waste of paper for him. He always maintained a copy of all important research papers and designs on his personal email ID. When the CEO was screaming at him in the chamber and calling him names, Lenkesh was deleting his work folder permanently from the laptop.

Thereafter, he pressed the latch to release the hard drive of the laptop and kept it securely in his pocket. He could not allow his research to be used by those who ousted him from the organisation. Then he took out a used hard drive from his drawer and replaced it with the original one before moving to the conference hall. The used hard drive had inconsequential official data on it, just the routine information.

Meanwhile, he had sent a message to his private lab's IT team. They sent large ping data packets (larger than the maximum allowable size) at his IP address, attempting a ping of death attack (a type of Denial of Service attack). The huge data load crashed his laptop.

He was now out of the office building. The Beadon Street at Lalpura bore a deserted look as Lenkesh looked at NODO for the last time. "The game changer Trinetra will bring all of you on your knees. Just wait and watch. Soon, it is going to be payback time."

First, he thought of going to Atrin's house. "No, I should not involve him in all this; police might be keeping an eye on his home. My son's name should not be dragged into all this. I have always been his hero, and such ignominy would shatter him." Lost in his thoughts, he sat in the bus.

He didn't even notice that the bus number 141 had started moving. Banna, the conductor, shook his shoulders and asked for the place to which he needed a ticket. Lenkesh murmured, for the last stop and handed him a five hundred rupee note.

Banna looked at him inquisitively. Who gives such a big note for a twenty rupee ticket? Is he crazy, or else he does not have a smaller denomination note? Whatever be the reason, Banna looked for the change in his bag. Luckily, he had the change. He returned the extra money and again looked at the person wearing such an expensive suit and travelling to the last stop - Tarulia, a small village near Panch Mukhi. So strange!

Banna got down at Beria Chowk bus stand as his shift had ended. Before alighting from the bus, he glanced at the affluently dressed passenger, who still looked lost.

Inside NODO, all hell had broken loose. No hard copies, no printed material, nothing of importance was found in his room. There were various prototype designs of submersibles in the office, but none of Trinetra. The internal security team remained empty-handed even after various efforts. Lenkesh had been a part of this organisation for long and knew well how the security teams operated. He had covered up his tracks well.

Just like her office colleagues, Chandrasi, too, had been a fan of Lenkesh and was initially shocked by his unceremonious ouster. But the CEO's revelations came as a jolter to her. She was appalled to know that in the last few years, NODO was being used as a plank by Lenkesh to promote himself. He was actually running a parallel set-up in the office as a one-man show. He cared a hoot for the organisation, and this dual nature was exposed after his sudden exit.

"I don't intend to overwhelm you with the enormity of the task at hand," said the CEO, "But it is my responsibility to warn you, don't take Lenkesh's expulsion lightly. He knows all the rule-books of NODO. He is well aware of our strengths and weaknesses as well as our standard protocols for dealing with crises. He is not done and dusted yet and might bounce back ferociously. It would be premature to write him off, and hence, you must act fast on building your defences against him. The central team is on its way and will be joining you in an hour."

"Our preliminary investigations reveal that Lenkesh was using security overrides in the system to mask his activities. Behind his façade of hard work lay a schemer who exploited the loopholes in the system to the hilt. He took the organisation for a ride and pricked at our vulnerabilities.

Don't worry; we are overhauling our systems to prevent future incidents. An inquiry has also been initiated against the Central Data System Administrator to probe his involvement. We should have seen it coming. Heads might roll at board level, too."

Dr Chandrasi was now well seized of the situation and knew that she would have to devise out of box strategies. Time was running out for Lenkesh. The next day was Purnima. Had he chosen that day for retaliation?

She was aware that, as an insider, Lenkesh knew all the technologies at NODO. She did not have anything innovative to offer on that front. But in this battle of nerves, complacency could be Lenkesh's weakest link and flabbergasting her strongest. She kept her fingers crossed.

Lenkesh, the senior scientist of NODO, was now a fugitive on the run. The police were frantically looking for him, but he seemed to have disappeared into thin air. Plain-clothes policemen were positioned outside Atrin's house also. There were strict instructions from head office that no news should leak out till Lenkesh was captured. Looking at the sensitivity of the matter, Dr Chandrasi's appointment was also kept under wraps.

Meanwhile, Lenkesh had finalised the programme with his angel investor. The stage was set for the final act. But father's heart was longing to hear his son's voice.

He switched on his mobile and told Atrin that he would be away for a few days. Atrin did not suspect anything unusual as Lenkesh generally worked continuously for days to meet his deadlines. "But Papa, next week is your birthday, and I have invited all your old friends to our beach house at Harekrishna Nagar." "Don't worry, I will be there on time," said Lenkesh.

Little did he realise that his phone was on surveillance, and unknowingly, he had given away his location. But then, Lenkesh was a doting father. He always spoke to Atrin before big projects. And tomorrow was perhaps the biggest day in his career! Whatever happened tomorrow, Lenkesh knew that his position was secured in history.

Dr Chandrasi was looking at the recent footage of the shafts near the ocean bed. They were placed close together, divided by only a couple of feet. But at their bases, a considerable amount of gallery work had been excavated. "Oh My God, this must have been done by the illegal miners who came after the people who originally sank the shafts!" Chandrasi now knew the exact location. "He is going to attack tomorrow," she shouted with alacrity.

Autonomous Underwater Vehicles (AUVs) were her best option. They were built to resist extreme pressures and low temperatures. These AUV's had been specifically designed for tough operating conditions particularly the pitch dark deep oceans.

Samudra yatris (the code name for AUVs) had a special mechanism to control its buoyancy to prevent it from sinking. They had four thrusters, two for propelling while the remaining two were for controlling its depth. She asked her team to double-check the cameras placed at the front of the Samudra yatris. They were going to be the eyes and ears of her team. Live feed of the operation was crucial for the control room at NODO as they knew that Lenkesh was waiting in ambush with his surreptitious attack plan.

She had designed her underwater chakravyuh[33] with multiple layers of attack. The coordination amongst these layers was critical as underwater navigation is often more complicated than aerial navigation. Firstly, poor underwater visibility; secondly, the absorption of radio waves by water; and finally, the risk of being hit by the large sharks many times creates hurdles in effective navigation.

The Samudra yatris were programmed by her team to use their onboard sensors. These acoustic sensors could reduce

---

[33] *a military formation comprising of seven layers of soldiers where weak and strong warriors are strategically placed in each of the layers, either to impose maximum damage on the opposing warriors or to defend the attacks from highly skilled enemy warriors.*

the complications of underwater navigation. Her attack plan included black spots, the colour-changing Samudra yatris. Their job was to be on standby in case the original one got hit either by the enemy or by a shark.

Lenkesh was in the submersible – Trinetra that fateful Purnima night when Samudra yatris began their attack. The beeping of sonar alarms startled Lenkesh. How did they track him? How did they get his exact location? He had no time to think as the Samudra yatris were getting closer. He initiated the dodge button; it gave him a breather of sixty seconds as swirling water jets hid his exact location.

He tried taking alternative exit routes, but Chandrasi had positioned Samudra yatris everywhere. Sensing no way out, he decided to take the plunge and began his descent deeper into the ocean. Lenkesh knew that the NODO AUVs were programmed to reduce their speed in descent. This could give him some time to plan his next move.

But he had underestimated Chandrasi. She had positioned Samudra yatris near the ocean bed, too, and they began their ascent as the target came closer. Lenkesh was now sandwiched between the twin attacks,one from the bottom and the other from the top. He could have escaped in the emergency pod of Trinetra and saved his life.

But then Trinetra would be captured by the National Oceanic Defence Organization. No, he would never let that happen. He would not let them take credit for his years of research.

He still had an ace in his hand - Trinetra's deadly weapon, 'Ternion'. But to balance the load on Trinetra, he had carried only one Ternion. And it was not enough. He should have planned to augment his weapon system. Clearly, he had not expected so many visitors tonight. With his back against the wall, Lenkesh was staring at defeat.

But surrender had never been a word in his vocabulary. He knew there was just one option. If he goes down, so goes his research, findings and his masterpiece Trinetra. With a heavy heart, Lenkesh, the creator of Trinetra, decided to destroy it. He reached for the backup files and pressed the Send button, followed by Auto Delete. Then he fired Ternion. Its roar could be heard up to miles away. Within a few seconds, numerous funnels erupted from the ocean bed, resulting in complete mayhem.

Dr Chandrasi's lightweight HIT missiles had fired, too. Their job was well cut as their target was Trinetra and its owner, Lenkesh. The firepower illuminated the water as if some chaotic laser show was on display inside the ocean.

The natural bioluminescence of the ocean was overshadowed for some time by this brutal display of firepower as Lenkesh embraced his water kingdom with open arms for the last time. His only solace was that Trinetra was going down with him. No one could ever touch Trinetra again; it was his baby. They lived together, and even death could not do them part.

Soon, the debris of Trinetra lay on the seabed, and the Samudra yatris began relaying live pictures of the wreckage. All of it was expeditiously retrieved from the sea bed. Scientists at the NODO lab were looking for information and data, but it looked like a dead end. They were trying again and again, searching for encrypted or coded messages, but remained empty-handed. All they had was the last mail sent to ss@xyz.com.

The Ternion attack by Lenkesh created a multiplier effect in the deep ocean and engulfed Panch Mukhi. The hapless residents ran helter-skelter but did not have a ghost of a chance to save themselves. The residents thought that a behemoth Anaconda had awoken in the ocean on the Purnima night to swallow the beautiful Panch Mukhi isles during the Purno Sindhu festival.

Even in his death, Lenkesh had blood on his hands.

Part III

Beware of Shark Kothi,
The Ouroboros is watching.....

XIII

SP and Atrin arrived in the national capital by a special chartered flight on a cold Monday morning in November 2022. It was an SOS call from their dear friend Mamak. He had called an urgent meeting to discuss measures to quell the dissidence in his Jan Sampark party. It was not an organic dissent which could be resolved through internal means. This time, his opponents were involved in chicanery to lure away a chunk of his MLAs(Member of Legislative Assembly). The fissures of dissent and disquiet in his party had been precipitated by his opponents with an eye on upcoming elections.

"So you want to keep your hands clean while we do the dirty work," said SP, winking at him. "Don't worry; I will take care of your problems. There are two ways to tackle this issue, either by money power or by muscle power. I have plenty of both. I will be generous with your MLAs and let them choose between the two. I hope they choose the non-violent money-power option!"

Atrin had a hearty laugh; some people and their ways never change. "SP, you have a quick-fix solution for everything. See, Mamak is looking so relieved now! Within a few seconds, you resolved the issue."

"SP is actually your Genie, Mamak. Whether it is arranging funds for your election campaigns or managing your dummy companies, SP always does the heavy lifting." Mamak nodded in agreement and smiled gently at Atrin's comment. In the last two decades Mamak has changed a lot, just like the river's journey from source to mouth. In the beginning, he possessed the purity and freshness of a river at its source .But on his way to success, the rules were flouted frequently. Rivers do get polluted by the dumping of untreated sewage and industrial waste on their way to mouth! Mamak's style too changed. The courage to speak against wrongdoings gradually waned, particularly if the overall results were beneficial.

"But I must say your Rainbow City project is a great idea," said SP while sipping the special tea in Mamak's office. Shifting the villagers from Sona Ghaati is crucial for us as it would give us unhindered access to the area. The dense forests would be a great location for our production facilities too as it provides natural cover and protection from the prying agencies. Its proximity to the ocean is greatly advantageous as it reduces our transportation costs. Once we gain control over TECHSIKA, there will be a seamless supply of money in our vaults. Our coffers will never be dry."

"Yes," said Atrin, "the success of our project depends on the swiftness with which the villagers vacate the area, and time is of the essence here. We tried talking with them and offered them money, but none of it worked. We cannot sit idle and twiddle our thumbs and wait for them to move out. I think it is time to release the virus. It spreads rapidly, and the villagers would panic for sure."

"A bio attack on our own people?" Mamak's voice quivered, "I thought our bio labs were production facilities that export to our overseas clients."

"Of course, it is meant for exports only, said SP. "Had the villagers moved out from the Sona Ghaati on their own free will, we would not have used the virus against them. They have forced this upon themselves."

"Have you thought about the media attention that this virus outbreak will create?" Asked Mamak.

"Don't worry. Once the virus is released, our men will spread the rumour that it is a curse of Sona Ghaati and if anyone tells the outsiders, the curse will befall their entire family. Rumours consume and spread like wildfire and hence, no news will leak out."

"But what about the proposed resort? Won't the continuous influx of tourists disturb our plan?" Mamak asked.

"Ah, the resort is a mere pretence to divert attention from Sona Ghaati's displacement. Our plan is to build production facilities at Sona Ghaati and not a tourist resort. We are pumping so much money into this. We deserve a good return on our investments."

"Once this frenzy dies down, we will deal with it. Our friend in Shark Kothi has a plethora of venomous snakes. I think we could use them," said Atrin. "The agencies will never give clearance to the resort if the security of the tourists is in danger."

"Don't you think that I should be funding the Rainbow City Project?" asked SP, looking at his friends. "It could help in boosting my image. The reporting of recent financial fiascos in the media has created a bit of negativity around me. As a public figure, I should be sensitive about public perception.

Maybe the news of funding this project could change that sentiment," said SP aloud.

Both Atrin and Mamak's faces lit up as they readily agreed to his proposal.

Quid Pro Quo was the name of the game. SP's funding for the Rainbow City Project led to his company being awarded the elite contract for the underground tunnel of the Khattrii Dam Canal project. With many of his companies being in the news for the wrong reasons, at least he had something to cheer about.

And he was right! The news of his funding the Rainbow City project for the upliftment of marginalised people spread like wildfire. After all, perceptions are not meant to be constant in the experiment called life.

The underground tunnel was to be built from Khattrii Dam on the Kohiari River to Ladati. It was the first time that SP's company was awarded the contract for an underground tunnel project. They didn't have any prior experience in such projects. Yet they beat some of the established firms in the business. Some eyebrows were raised, but none had the guts to speak against the mighty SP.

The contract, too, had its share of twists and turns. Initially, the Chief Executive was furious. "So, are you telling me that such a big project can be awarded to a first-timer with no experience? It is against the rules, don't you know that? I am not going to sign it." He threw the file back at the junior officer.

"Sir, every firm is a first-timer once; look at these top companies. They also needed their first contract to rise to the pinnacle," said his junior in a subdued tone. Now, how could one say no to such an argument, particularly when the Chief Executive was being offered a penthouse in a posh area! The officer's conscience withered under the weight of the penthouse.

SP then subcontracted the excavation part to a small-time contractor, Dhokba, who readily agreed at almost the basic cost price. The agreement papers were discussed and given to him for getting printed in two copies. "Get it printed from Robo Associates. Just take our firm's name, and they will do it for free." Although Dhokba knew other printers in the area, none would do it for free. The next day, Dhokba, dressed in his best clothes, reached SP's office with the printed agreement papers. He had never seen such a plush office and was thanking his stars for the offer that was bound to change his life.

"I have a meeting with SP," said Dhokba. The guard looked at him with disdain and then picked up the intercom. "What is your name?" asked the guard.

Dhokba was still in awe of the surroundings and couldn't pay heed to the guard repeating his question. At that very instant, SP entered and apologised to Dhokba for the delay. "Come with me," said SP and asked his personal staff to bring Dhokba's bag. Dhokba was on cloud nine as the capsule lift's door closed.

Soon, they entered the chamber, and Dhokba was offered tea by SP's secretary. He was super excited to be sitting next to the double-glazed large window, sipping tea with SP in the elegantly designed office.

Both copies of the agreement were signed by Dhokba and SP. Dhokba still could not believe that he was sitting in front of one of the richest businessmen in the country.

"I have an important meeting in ten minutes," said SP as he shook hands with Dhokba and exited in a hurry. "Sir is very busy these days. I would say, you are fortunate to have a personal meeting with him," the secretary said in a hushed voice.

He then offered sweets to Dhokba, welcoming him to the SP Empire. "Start your work today itself, and here is your advance." Dhokba had never seen so much cash in his life. He collected the cash and his copy of the agreement and thanked the secretary. As Dhokba came down, the guard saluted him. In a few hours, from nobody, he seemed to have become somebody!

Back in the chamber, the secretary was looking closely at the agreement papers signed by Dhokba. It had been redrafted by SP's legal team with variations, which understandably suited SP's company. And it goes without saying that it had the golden line, "In case of any dispute, this copy would be treated as original and would be binding on all parties".

Actually, Robo Associates, the printing firm, had a long relationship with SP. They had a standard format and design for agreements related to SP's firm. As soon as the client approached them for agreement printing, they sent one soft copy to SP's secretary along with the invoice. Their bills were realised immediately, and that alone mattered to them. Once the original agreement was received, SP's legal team made the requisite changes, and the secretary took care of the rest.

Sub-contracting was an industry norm, and as per SP, he was helping these small-time contractors. "How else would they get exposure? They should be thanking me for getting work in such prestigious projects," he often said.

He had instructed his team to never repeat any subcontractor. They always selected new ones and exploited their vulnerability. In case anyone dared to speak, SP used the threat of getting them blacklisted.

The secretary slid the tabletop, took out the original agreement papers brought by Dhokba, and put them in the shredder. He had replaced the papers while Dhokba was enjoying the moment near the window, relishing his tea. Poor Dhokba, will he ever find out the cost of that cup of tea!

The seemingly invincible troika of SP, Mamak and Atrin was having a dream run. SP and Mamak had been friends for more than two decades; Atrin joined them a few years later and occupied his father's place. Initially, SP had Lenkesh and Mamak as partners, but everything changed after December 2004. They were forced to lie low for some time as NODO's investigations were going on. But it was Atrin's entry that prompted them to revive Lenkesh's dream a few years later.

Over the years, they had penetrated rather permeated into the system so well that they were now omnipresent from the regulatory bodies to the sports associations and even as government nominees on various boards. The country was growing fast, and the trio ensured that their own growth was manifold times the national growth rate. Their offshore units were booming, with the proceeds coming via the healthy 'Hawala' route, as SP called it. And to add salt to the wounds of the common man, recently SP and Atrin were officially nominated for the think tank committee on 'Checks and Balances for clean money strategy'!

To strengthen their empire, the famous Nabinagar triad opened its doors a few years ago for sand mafia Durjan, turning them into the fearsome foursome. Initially, Mamak was against the idea of letting fugitive Durjan in, but SP insisted. "See, it is not a scramble for power; it is all about what power can do. Durjan brings new skill sets to our table, and his association will surely take us to new heights." And SP's words proved true again and again.

SP's associate company, 'The Rising Sun', had taken a loan from a five-bank consortium and was now facing insolvency. The NPA (non-performing assets) in the loan account of 'The Rising Sun' had mounted to more than Rs. fifteen thousand crores. To add to his woes, the fund diversion charge against the company was also being probed by the National Companies Board.

But then, a friend in need is a friend indeed. 'Grey Gilt', the front company of Mamak, having no relevant experience and negligible net worth, turned out to be the highest bidder in the auction for SP's troubled company. Mamak's Grey Gilt sealed the deal with the winning bid of Rs. four hundred twenty crores.

A double toast was raised for Durjan, the ideator and implementer. It was his two-in-one role that saved SP from financial turbulence. "How do you manage it?" Atrin asked.

"Ito Bhrashtah tato Bhrashtah (*Unethical Here, Unethical There*)," Durjan responded with a wicked smile.

Atrin needed a free hand in ocean research and mining explorations. "I don't want any interference or disturbances. It was my father's kingdom, and I will rule it again," said Atrin forcefully. SP readily agreed to this proposal as Atrin had promised to take care of investigative agencies probing the money laundering charges in SP's non-banking financial company named, 'Hope for All'.

The money laundering activities would have continued unabated had it not been for Madhab, the RTI (Right to Information) activist. Two attempts were made on his life, but that did not deter him from pursuing the truth. He persistently kept asking questions, and soon 'hope (LESS) for All' began to trend on social media. The print media, too, lent its weight to the activist, and soon, the news became too hot to handle.

The regulatory authorities took cognizance and immediately ordered a thorough probe into the company, 'Hope for All'. When the Know Your Customer (KYC) documents were checked by the regulatory authorities, more than twenty per cent of them were found to be in the names of deceased persons.

These were literally ghost accounts in which huge numbers of transactions were happening. Small deposits (below fifty thousand) were made in cash, then layered and finally integrated into the system. The entries seemed to be intentionally kept at Rs. forty-nine thousand nine hundred or below to escape the regulatory net, and the money was then conveniently withdrawn through Automated Teller Machines.

The scenario looked bleak for the company as initial investigations pointed to a systemic and well-thought-out scam. The rot ran deep as the senior officers had conveniently overlooked the loopholes. The auditors, too, had turned a blind eye, and the company seemed to be operating in a no-rule land.

Loans had been given to the dead people and then written off in the bank books. Most of these account holders had their thumb impressions on the loan documents and none of them had been verified by the bank officers.

Atrin knew that it was an uphill task for any company to get away from these serious charges, so he dialled his secretary to get the probe slowed down. "My team is trying to get an extension of at least six months for submitting the investigation report," said Atrin. "Don't worry, people will forget this scam in some time. Lengthy investigations are directly proportional to diminishing public interest in them. Moreover, neither 'Hope for All' is the first company nor 'The Rising Sun' is the last one to fail. Why should we panic when we have companies like 'Grey Gilt', which can buy these insolvent companies at peanut's price ?"

Their laughter resonated in Atrin's lavish farmhouse. In its din, it buried the cries of millions whose hard-earned money got appropriated. As they say in Latin, "Quis Custodiet Ipsos Custodes" (*who will guard the guards*)?

A month later, the soil of the underground canal collapsed. Ninety labourers were trapped inside as the under-construction tunnel of the Khattrii dam canal project caved in. The delayed response by the relief and rescue team angered the locals. They tried with hand axes and hatchets, but it was not enough that night. It didn't take much time for the media to understand that the flouting of safety protocols had led to the loss of lives of poor labourers.

SP's connections with top brass ensured that the blame was put on lower-level staff. The state machinery swung into action, albeit late and announced compensation. But no one spoke about accountability.

Dhokba had asked for the land subsidence reports before commencing work, but SP's team laughed away his apprehensions. "Sir, land subsidence occurred in the area last year; it is risky. Can't we just skirt the troubled section for now and redesign the route of the underground canal?" Dhokba had asked.

With his spectacle resting on the tip of the nose, SP's secretary gave him a hard look. "Do you have any idea how much your proposal for route change is going to cost? And who is going to foot its bill? Remember one thing: SP Sir's word is the law. If he has given the go-ahead to this project, there will not be an iota of change. This is your first time with SP Sir. I hope you don't want to make it your last one."

Not raising your voice is a vice; Dhokba learnt this lesson the hard way as his worst fears came true on the ill-fated evening. "The collapse was not a natural disaster.It could have been averted. Rather it was a man-made accident waiting to happen." But who would lend an ear to a small-time contractor's word against the real estate big-shot SP?

His conscience forced him to step out of the house and speak the truth. SP's musclemen, who were keeping vigil outside his house, followed him. As Dhokba turned right on the road to the Police Station, a truck came out of nowhere and knocked him down. His lifeless body lay battered on the road to justice!

Nonetheless, within a fortnight, the Court took suo moto cognizance of the Khattrii dam canal project mishap and posted it for an emergency hearing. SP was caught unawares; it had never happened before.

Brainstorming sessions by SP's legal team and top lawyers converged on his next move. They suggested to him in unison to not contest the liability as public anger was very high on this emotive issue. The heart-wrenching visuals of the mangled bodies of the labourers had stirred protests across various states. Mamak's closeness to SP meant that political rivals could soon be gunning for him also. Both Atrin and Mamak seemed to agree with the legal team's suggestion to surrender.

"Shyam Pradosh and surrender, impossible!" Thundered the powerful magnate as his fist hit the table. "I believe in Lilliputian media, subdued courts and a rubber stamp legislature. Any kind of activism weakens this ecosystem. My surrender would send a wrong signal to our opponents. I can't afford to appear weak at this juncture."

My opponents are underestimating my power.I have amassed wealth and power over the years, and the authorities bow before me. And you people are telling me that this trivial incident dares to question my supremacy? Rules are meant to be circumvented, and there are people who will do it readily for me.

"I don't believe in multiple layers of power as 'too many cooks often spoil the broth.' Just offer something huge to the dealing person, something that he or she has never dreamt of." As SP spoke agitatedly, he looked around the room for support, but none nodded. Atrin, Mamak, and the legal team were all sitting with their heads down as if prodding him to accept the inevitable.

"Sir, it won't take more than an hour," his team pleaded. "Our legal team will get you bail in no time. We will proceed after breakfast and be back by lunch."

He looked at his daughter Mugdha, who was trying hard to control her emotions. He could do anything to bring a smile to her face. She was his biggest achievement and meant the world to him. SP was so proud of his daughter. She was the one who could easily stand as a wall against his detractors, whether inside the courtroom or outside it.

"Okay, let's do it on the fifteenth of March, the day after the inauguration of Rainbow Conclave," SP said. All of them heaved a sigh of relief as the legal team began the paperwork.

XIV

The morning incident at the hotel had delayed Kraman's departure by about an hour. "I hope to reach there in time," he thought, looking at the watch. The driver, observed his action in the rear mirror, and said smilingly, "You seem to be new to this place.Are you late for something?" "Yes," said Kraman, "I need to reach gate number seven of the Rainbow Conclave by eleven a.m."

"Sir, there is a shortcut to Loka. Instead of going through the main city, we will take the state highway and then pass through Maharaja Shakti Shubhankar's estate. By the way, Loka is the old name of Rainbow City. The old residents prefer calling it by that name only.There is some big businessman named SP,he is funding this new township. Tomorrow they are having a grand programme at Rainbow Conclave. Have you also come for that programme?"

Kraman smiled affirmatively and relaxed into the deluxe back seat. The villagers of Sona Ghaati being provided pucca houses in the Rainbow City was a revelation. But why is a canny businessman like SP funding this township?

"SP and empathy do not go together; rather, they have a south-pole-north-pole relationship. He belongs to that genre where empathy is considered a deterrent for power aspirants. Helping the village folks is certainly not his cup of tea. The real estate bigwig agreeing to invest money in Rainbow City points to some behind-the-scenes deliberations.Something's cooking," mused Kraman.

Soon, they were crossing through an undisturbed meadow, a place with no Wi-Fi, and as he looked out of the window, he felt an instant connection with the ethereal surroundings. The flock of flying birds against the backdrop of breathtakingly blue sky and the whistling winds complemented the picturesque setting.

"Should I switch on the AC (air conditioner)?" The driver asked. Kraman waved his hand in negative and continued to inhale the fresh oxygen and enjoy the scenic bounty. Nature makes us feel so very alive and kicking; it is indeed a priceless experience.

"Sir, the whole area on the right side of the road belonged to Maharaja." He slowed down a bit to show the estate. Kraman could see the contours of a dense forest far away. That is the Sona Ghaati.

"We have been living here for ages. Maharaja never objected, but these Rainbow City officials are bent upon driving us out of our homes. They have promised to give us houses in lieu of our homes. But tell me, sir, is it a fair deal? Can these moneyed men buy the freshness of the air or the sparkle of water? Can they own the mist in the woods or the warmth of the land? Soon, these springs will be gone forever." His voice quivered as tears brimmed in his eyes. "We are being forced to sell our lands, but when no one owns nature, how can one buy it?"

Kraman had no answers as he looked wistfully out of the window at the bountiful natural surroundings. "Sir, there is a special tea shop around the corner. You won't get such tea anywhere in the world," said the driver. "Okay, let's stop for a while," Kraman concurred. Soon, the car stopped near the 'famous tea shop' as described by the driver. "Bring masala chai [34], Vicky," said the driver, looking at the boy. Kraman raised two fingers, one tea for the driver, too.

It was a small shop, but there seemed to be a gathering near it. Kraman could hear animated discussions about the Rainbow City project. Some of the youngsters seemed to be on board as it envisaged opportunities for them. The elderly were hesitant, understandably so. They were pained at the thought of having to leave their forefather's lands.

But the crowd as a whole was very angry with the Rainbow City Project as it was forcing them to leave not only their homes but also their forests and rivers.

Even his driver joined them and was seemingly preoccupied with the discussion. There was another group speaking about Kamtej, the famous Lawyer. They were agitated about the protest march at Sona Ghaati and the rally at Fauz Maidan being abruptly cancelled by the administration.

Vicky was soon there with the tea in an earthen cup. He was wearing a blue shirt which had only two buttons. Kraman asked, "What happened to your buttons?" "It was a fistfight," said Vicky sheepishly, "Yesterday, there was a movie show at the village council building, the first ever to be held at Loka. There was a lot of jostling to get inside, but only the lucky ones managed to get in."

---

[34] *spiced tea*

"So what are you unhappy about, not being able to see the movie or the bragging of your friends who watched it?" Asked Kraman playfully. "Both," said Vicky in a downcast tone, "You know my next-door neighbour Lucky also got a chance to get inside, but not me."

"Do you like chocolates," asked Kraman?

Was the question for providing solace to him or a bribe to continue his story? Tough to say, as Vicky was initially hesitant but took the chocolate after a bit of cajoling. He looked at the owner of the stall, who was still actively engaged in conversation with people around his shop.

"So you have never seen a movie?" Asked Kraman.

"Once, I went to the city with my father. They have big movie halls there, bigger than our village council building," said Vicky with his eyes wide open, "But you know they ask for a lot of money to get in. You have to buy tickets," he said like a wise man. "The cost of one ticket is more than my one month's salary here at the tea shop. But maybe these Rainbow City people will soon make a movie hall here!"

Kraman looked in his pockets for some more chocolates, but he had none. "Wait, I have it in my backpack." As he handed over the entire box of chocolate bars, this time, Vicky took it instantly. "Take my handkerchief to cover your chocolates," said Kraman smilingly.

"I will keep them in my pocket, he said, refusing the handkerchief. I never had anything this delicious; it is so soft yet crunchy. How is it made?" Asked Vicky. "Once I grow up, I will make these chocolates for my friends."

"Friends!" Winked Kraman, "But they fought with you yesterday!" "Oh yes!" There was an angry look on Vicky's face, but soon an innocent smile took over. Perhaps the flicker of anger had been doused by the gentle stream of friendship.

"Do you see these people?" Asked Vicky, looking at Kraman pensively. Many of them had faces semi-covered with towels; even his driver had a cap and a muffler. Most of them were wearing full shirts or kurta or had a shawl draped around them. "One day, I will also become like them," Vicky's voice sounded grim for the first time.

The shopkeeper was coming towards them. As he came closer, Kraman made the payment. "How was the tea, Sir?" He asked, "Hope Vicky did not bother you much."

"The tea was very refreshing, and Vicky's stories were like icing on the cake," said Kraman. "The spices in tea, particularly the cardamom, energised me completely. Thank you, Kaka."

As the shopkeeper turned back, he stumbled and fell down. Kraman picked up the shawl and turned to give it back to the shopkeeper. And then he froze. The shopkeeper had blisters all over his body, with pus oozing out of it. For a moment, he closed his eyes in fear and then regained composure and helped the shopkeeper with the shawl. He muttered something and raced back to the shop.

"All of us have it. It is the curse of Sona Ghaati. None will be spared." Vicky's words were now sounding like a grim prophecy, "We are prohibited from speaking to outsiders about this. The disease is spreading and the only way to save ourselves is to leave Sona Ghaati. We are not supposed to show our blisters. See, small blisters have started coming on my knees, too."

As Kraman drew close, some sand from his handkerchief fell on Vicky's knee. "What is the soothing powder you put on my knee? See, the redness of blisters has dimmed, and the pain has also eased a bit," said Vicky.

"Ah, it is the effect of chocolates. I will send you another box soon," said Kraman, scurrying towards the waiting cab. The driver smiled at him, but this time, Kraman's response was feeble. He could feel the pain, the helplessness and the angst of the driver. The cab soon resumed its journey.

His mind was in a fix. How did the sand-like material have such a therapeutic effect on the blisters? It was definitely not sand. But why was it delivered in the envelope to him? Was the attack on the hotel related to the sand-like material in the envelope?

"We are about to reach," the driver's voice broke his chain of thoughts. He took out Rs. five hundred from the wallet and sprinkled a little bit of sand in its fold. Then he handed the note to the driver in a way that the sand fell on his blistered palms. The driver immediately closed his palm lest the blisters be visible. "Thank you," said Kraman, praying earnestly that the sand would ease his pain and suffering.

Decked up with flowers and hoardings of PENAK Associates, the venue of Rainbow Conclave looked seemingly appropriate for a wedding. "Most of the guests seemed to have stayed in Nabinagar. Tomorrow, there is bound to be a traffic jam-like situation near the venue," thought Kraman.

He was near the main gate as he looked at the watch. He still had fifteen minutes to reach gate number seven.

The local residents seemed amused as well as perplexed by this sudden rush of people. The potholes of the roads had disappeared overnight. Fogging machines had been deployed at main points to fight the mosquito menace. A temporary helipad was readied for VIPs like heavyweight politician Mamak Vragji, real estate baron SP and business tycoon Atrin Kumar.

The deserted look of Fauz Maidan stood in dark contrast to the Rainbow Conclave venue, which was bustling with people. The Rainbow Conclave was shimmering with festivities, whereas the Maidan lay still with just a handful of guards.

The condition of the two places was like a see-saw. The organisers of Rainbow Conclave lay low when the protesters assembled yesterday at the Fauz Maidan. During the day, the protesters were forcibly evicted. Fauz Maidan bore the signs of a struggle between the police and supporters of Kamtej. As the Maidan was silenced, the festivities became boisterous at the Rainbow Conclave.

It was clear both could not go hand in hand.

Sitting alone in the secluded guest house, Kamtej was taken aback at the coincidence of events. In 2001, as a young lawyer, he was fighting for Victor, the then CM Sitara Devi's son's friend, who had gone missing after the infamous farmhouse drug raid. Hon'ble Supreme Court, on his habeas corpus petition, had ordered the state government to produce Victor within forty-eight hours. 'The Courts coming to the rescue of the common man', 'Justice delivered', and many such headlines had hogged the newspapers at that time.

And today, he was in a similar condition, in waiting mode for some kind of intervention. His phone, laptop and books had been taken away. Yesterday, after a lot of discussions, the administration allowed him to sit on dharna in the Fauz Maidan under the watchful eyes of the police. The media was not permitted to even come near Fauz Maidan. Most of his supporters were taken into preventive custody. In the night, he was taken to a hotel, and since morning, he was confined in this windowless small room, which seemed to have been painted lately as the smell of fresh paint was still there. He had been inside the room for quite some time now.

And then, to add to his woes, there was a power cut. Kamtej hung his head in exasperation in the pitch-dark room. As he tried to adjust his eyes to the surrounding darkness, there was a glow on the wall. The rare green colour petals, with red dots gleamed on the wall, "Ah, it is the phosphorescence[35] effect!"

As he drew closer, he could see the painting of the Gold of Kinabalu orchids. Being a nature enthusiast , Kamtej has been to various famous parks. The National Kinabalu Park Malaysia was one of his favourites, where he had seen these exceptionally beautiful orchids.

"But who drew this painting here, and why was the wall freshly painted? Was it done to cover the orchid painting?" Suddenly, the door opened, and the caretaker entered with his

---

[35] *the glowing of a painting after being charged with the room light*

things. "Sir, a car is waiting for you outside. It will take you directly to the Nabinagar Airport. Here are your personal belongings and some fresh fruits from the garden."

The caretaker bowed to touch Kamtej's feet. "I know you are Maharaja's son; please forgive me. I was just obeying orders. The place has changed a lot since you left," murmured the caretaker as he opened the door of the car. "I am so sorry, the room was shabby. I got it painted yesterday only. There is an old gardener here who keeps on drawing flowers on the walls. I have never seen such flowers in my life. I think the gardener is a daydreamer."

Kamtej checked his mobile for messages, and one of them brought an instant smile to his face. The Hon'ble Court had accepted the Sona Ghaati PIL[36] and listed it for the fifteenth of March.

---

[36] *Public Interest Litigation*

XV

Kraman was eagerly waiting at gate number seven for his mysterious sponsor. A lot had happened in the last twenty-four hours. "Firstly a failed plane hijack and then a blast-like situation near Moksha Hotel, a puzzle written in invisible ink and people suffering from some abstruse illness at the tea shop and someone breaking into his hotel room to steal the sand-like material. This looks like a jigsaw puzzle with a few missing pieces," thought Kraman. Suddenly, a small boy came running to him with a fresh coconut and a straw. "Maali[37] Kaka has given this," pointing towards an old man sitting under the tree.

The coconut water was so refreshing that Kraman went personally to thank the person sitting under the tree. He looked quite frail, and his head, as well as half his face, was covered with a shawl. Kraman thanked him and turned back to see if his sponsor had arrived.

"How is Suchita? Hope she is doing well," asked the old man. Now, this question startled Kraman. "But how do you know her?" "Well, I had been to her house at Chandinagar. Suchita's family had to face social banishment for no fault of theirs," said the old man. Now, that surprised Kraman more. He moved closer to see the face of the gardener. "Yes, that was very painful for

---

[37] *gardener*

Suchita didi, but how are you connected to Chandinagar?" Asked Kraman, "What are you doing here?"

"I am Suyash, the person who invited you to Nabinagar. I will answer all your questions. But not here, come with me. Let's go home first. But tell me one thing, Kraman, aren't you disappointed to see an old man as your host?" Getting no answers, he trudged slowly towards his house. "Ah, there it is, 'my humble abode'," he said with an intended pun in his voice. Kraman could not stop smiling at his sense of humour.

On their way, they met the caretaker, who was livid at Suyash. "I have told you so many times not to draw on the walls, but you never listen. One day, I am going to lose my job because of you." Suyash merely smiled and promised not to draw on the walls again, but Kraman could see a sparkle in his eyes as he glanced at his wall painting with pride.

He unlocked the door and asked Kraman to sit on the cane chair as he sat on the bed to catch his breath. It was a small room and a bit dingy, too. It seemed as if the bed sheet and the pillow had not been cleaned for a long time. After resting for a bit, he began digging into his pillow. A bemused Kraman kept watching him from the chair.

Finally, Suyash got hold of something and took his hand out of the pillow. It was an envelope; he opened it slowly and handed over the contents to Kraman. There were a few sheets of paper with account numbers, bank addresses and company details.

And then Suyash dropped the bombshell, "Do you know the account numbers in the envelope pertain to Shyam Pradosh? Most people know him as a businessman. But behind this sanctimonious mask lies a bloodthirsty shark that devours its prey mercilessly. These documents are proof of how all this began at Nabinagar. Kali Babu was his first victim."

There was pin-drop silence in the room as Kraman looked at the details again. Some of these accounts are in Zurich, and a few are in the Cayman Islands and other places. "The names of shell companies running on his behalf are on the backside," said Suyash.

"May I ask you a question, Suyash Kaka? Why have you chosen me for this task? You don't even know me; we never met before. The person you have named just now is too powerful for me, and you know that well. The David vs Goliath battle outcomes vary in the real world, and by the way, what makes you believe that I will readily take him head on?"

"So many questions! Take a breath, son. Do you want more coconut water?"

"No, first answer my questions," Kraman said with a slightly bemused expression.

"Okay, let's start with your questions one by one. You remember Kraman, the series of articles that you had written against the free run of the sand mining mafia near your college?"I think you were an engineering student then. In one of the articles, you had written about the gruesome incident of a farmer's legs being crushed under the SUV[38] by the musclemen of the sand mafia. The farmer's crime was that he

---

[38] *Sports Utility Vehicle*

was going to the police station to report the sand mining operation. "The single-handed resolve resonating in your articles forced the local administration to take action against the illegal miners."

Honestly, I was amazed by your clarity of thought and strong conviction."Your intrinsic fearlessness seems to have powered your journey through adversities."I read your articles in prison and tried gathering information about you. I requested my kind-hearted jailor (who belonged to Chandinagar) to enquire about your background. He told me that you had been under the guidance of Suchita in your formative years.

I sent you this invitation knowing fully well that, coming from the land of Chanakya, you would aptly use his policies to checkmate Shyam Pradosh. "You must have read Mahabharata, where the five Pandavas won against the mighty Kauravas, who were more resourceful and had a bigger army." Do you know why? "Because the truth was with the Pandavas, and they were fighting for justice and not for any personal gains."

On their way to success, people like SP habitually trample people like Kali Babu, and their blood-laden footmarks point to a despicable narrative. "What angers me more is that such people conveniently exemplify their rags-to-riches stories and boast of determination and grit but conceal their tales of deceit and manipulation…"

Just then, a young police officer entered the room. "…He is Diganta, my confidante for years." Suyash's eyes were brimming with pride as he spoke about Diganta. He could still see the young boy selling newspapers beside the pavement on that rainy day. "Diganta knows a lot about this case and will be of immense help to you."

"Hi Diganta, haven't we met before at the Kedarkantha trek?" Asked a surprised Kraman. Yes, Suyash Kaka had asked me to accompany you on the trek. One of my friends was the tour organiser there, and as soon as he confirmed your booking, I blocked my dates too. But I must confess, you are an excellent hiker," said Diganta smilingly.

"I have arranged for your stay in the neighbouring guest house. Let Kaka rest for some time. He has been so very excited since you arrived here. Come, I will drop you there," said Diganta as he started his bike and signalled to Kraman. "The police station is about three kilometres from your guesthouse. Call me if you need anything. I usually bring Kaka's lunch at one p.m., and I will see you then."

Kraman called his office and shared the data with them. He was pacing in the guesthouse when his team called. To his chagrin, many of the bank accounts had been closed. His sources informed him that there appeared to be trails of money laundering in those closed accounts. However, there was one specific account in the name of Viraj, which was still operative and frequent transactions were taking place in that account through related accounts.

This morning, i.e. on the thirteenth of March itself, there had been a transfer of Rs. thirty lacs from SP's account to Viraj. Rather, Viraj was a frequent beneficiary of SP's largesse.

"That is surprising.Send me Viraj's photo immediately," Kraman told his cyber teammate.

"Sometimes there is a power cut, so it is better to keep the windows open," suggested the caretaker as he entered the room with a glass of lemonade. "Thanks," said Kraman as he looked at the beautifully curated garden once the caretaker opened the windows. Suyash Kaka had really maintained it well. The sound of notification diverted his attention as he turned towards the laptop.

A photo was downloading, and he was startled, to say the least. The similarities in three seemingly dissimilar people whom he had seen today was a strange coincidence. Lal Kunwar, whom he met in person at Nabinagar Airport; Durjan, whose pic he saw in the newspaper packing of Vada Pav and now this Viraj's photo. He immediately opened the photo editor app on his laptop.

Incidentally, he had folded the paper and kept it in his pocket after eating the world's 'best Vada Pav' in the morning, as there were no dustbins around. And as a Clean Beach activist, he could never add to the litter on the beach. This eco-friendly habit proved to be of great help today.

He uploaded Viraj's photo to the photo editor and began editing. First, he added the cut mark on his right forehead, and then imperial moustaches & ducktail beard (just as they were in newspaper wrapper) and saved the picture. He took the photo of Viraj again, added the red hat and sunglasses and saved it. Now, he opened the three pictures on one screen and ran the matching percentage software. It was a ninety per cent match.

He sank to the floor, still staring at his laptop in disbelief. "There is something more to this than meets the eye." Why did SP transfer such a huge amount to Viraj on the day the paternity suit's hearing was listed? Was Kavya's death on the previous night a random occurrence, a coincidence or a well-executed plan? His journalistic mind reminded him of Ian Fleming's quote, "Once is happenstance. Twice is coincidence. The third time it's enemy action.".

What was the purpose behind a single person donning three identities? Durjan, a sand mafia; Lal Kunwar, a flight passenger; and Viraj, an intermediary receiving payments. Kraman was baffled to see a sole person acting as three different people in three seemingly unconnected fields. Were these multiple identities of Viraj his own game plan, or was he acting at somebody's behest?

Kraman turned his head as there was a light, dignified knocking on the door. Diganta, pale as death, with his hands clasped in prayer, was standing in the scorching sun, glaring tragically into Kraman's eyes. "Suyash Kaka has been shifted to the ICU." The overhead timepiece tilted dangerously at the pressure of his head. He caught it with his trembling fingers and set it back in place. But the clock had stopped.

The last interaction was moving like a reel in front of Kraman's eyes as Suyash Kaka held his hand and said, "Suchita needs closure too. I am her culprit, as she had to pay the penalty for my fight with SP. I wanted justice for Kali Babu, but poor Suchita became collateral damage in this struggle. I keep thinking, what was her fault?"

The last question had been haunting Kraman for years. Why Suchita didi? Why had destiny been so cruel? He wiped his tears and put on his sunglasses as they were about to reach the hospital.

"He is on life support. The next twenty-four hours are going to be crucial," said the doctor in a grim tone. "Is he going to be okay?" both Kraman and Diganta asked in unison.

"We are trying our best, said the doctor, "but he is still unconscious." Kraman and Diganta held each other's hands tightly as they prayed silently for Suyash Kaka. 'No Visitors Allowed' sign was blinking outside the ICU as they moved to the waiting area.

"It was a tough time for him out there," said Diganta as he spoke about Kali Babu's death, SP's involvement and Suyash's incarceration. Tough physical conditions in prison, coupled with mental turmoil for being tainted a murderer and, above all, his failure to get SP behind bars, was too suffocating for Kaka.

"The mental burden was drowning him in an ocean of helplessness and grief. He seemed to be getting lonelier day by day. He even stopped talking to anyone and just kept staring at the prison walls. His deteriorating health conditions and frequent hospitalisations made him frailer," Diganta added in a quivering voice. "Each day spent in the prison added a year to his age. Just look at him; he looks almost double his age."

There were few prisoners pursuing the distance learning educational programmes who approached Suyash Kaka to help them in their studies. Initially, he declined but later relented on the jailor's insistence. Slowly, it became his motive in life as hopes of being released from prison receded day by day. Meanwhile, his classes rose in popularity amongst the prisoners.

Looking at his good conduct, the prison authorities recommended his application for remission. It took more than a year for his release orders to be issued. But his release did not help him much. He could neither recover from the mental trauma of Kali Babu's death nor the physical trauma that he had to undergo in prison.

By the time he came out of prison, Suyash Kaka had already been labelled as a villain in society. He did not have many visitors in the prison either."I was the only person with whom he has been in touch all these years," said Diganta. "After his release, he moved to this small town, Loka (now called Rainbow City) and started an anonymous life as a gardener. I had requested him to stay with me, but he declined. Very few people in this town even know his name. They all know him as a gardener who grows as well as paints beautiful flowers," said Diganta.

"Oh yes, very beautiful flowers, but tell me, has he ever been to Mt. Kinabalu? I saw his paintings of Kinabalu Gold – the rare species of the orchid on the walls in the guest house."

Diganta glanced back to check if someone was in the vicinity and then spoke in a hushed tone, "He told me once about it. A few days before Kali Babu's death, SP had shown him the Gold of Kinabalu painting that he had bought at an insane price in the auction. Basically, he wanted to show off by bragging about the exorbitantly priced painting."

Kudos to Suyash Kaka's eidetic memory; he could redraw the design flawlessly. I don't think he has ever been to Mt. Kinabalu, but his drawings are very lively and elegant," said Diganta with pride.

Since you asked about these orchids, I remember Suyash Kaka once telling me about the incident when he saw Siraj (Investigative Officer in Kali Babu's case) as the Chief Guest at the prison's Independence Day celebrations. He had become the Additional Superintendent of Police by then.

It was sheer chance that this photo fell from his pocket. When Kaka saw the photo, he immediately recalled SP's beautiful orchid flower painting adorning the wall. Against that backdrop, there were three people in the photo, along with SP. First was the young politician Mamak, then there was Viraj, and the third face was unclear. On the backside of the photograph, 'housewarming party @ SS' was written. Maybe the photo had been clicked by Siraj. When Kaka saw him looking for the photo, he dropped it to the ground and moved away. Had he got some more time, he could have tried to look closely at the unclear face!

"Well, I have something strange with me," said Kraman sharing the pictures of Viraj, Lal Kunwar and Durjan. "Have you met them before?"

"Well, the first one looks like Viraj," said Diganta. "He had come to my Police Station looking for Suyash Kaka. I think it was a few months after Kaka's release from prison. But why is he wearing these different attires?"

"Are you hundred per cent sure?" Kraman asked in a bewildered tone. "Yes, Suyash Kaka confirmed his name when I showed him the Police Station's CCTV footage.

"But how do you know Viraj?" It was Diganta's surprised voice, "And who are the other two lookalikes of Viraj?"

"Well, one of them was a fellow passenger on my flight to Nabinagar," said Kraman, "The second photo I found on the poster as a wanted criminal. And of course, the third one, Viraj is the account holder who received money from SP yesterday. Rather, he has been receiving money on a regular basis. Both seem to be close acquaintances"

"When I showed Viraj's photo to Suyash Kaka, he spoke nothing about this curious case of multiple identities." Diganta sounded angry.

"Maybe he wanted to protect you from danger. You know how deeply he loves you," said Kraman. Diganta nodded his head as he tried to hide his tears from Kraman. "I owe my life to him for saving my mother. On that rainy day, he seemed to have descended as a divine messenger in our lives and changed it forever. Every morning, when I touch my mother's feet, I thank Kaka. He is our saviour."

Kraman's eyes got misty as he thought of Suchita didi. She had chosen the right person as her life partner. Suyash Kaka and Suchita didi would have made a great couple. "It seems your phone is vibrating," said Diganta, looking at the phone kept on the side table near him. It was a call from NODO's office asking Kraman to board the black car waiting near the hospital gates. Kraman asked Diganta to be at the hospital till his return as he moved towards the gate.

Meeting Dr Chandrasi twice in two days was indeed a big surprise. "Good afternoon, ma'am," said Kraman. "I am your big fan. You are a role model for all of us. The way you staved off the hijackers yesterday it was incredible. But I still don't understand why an important dignitary like you chose to travel without security?"

"I am going to be the one asking questions, not you. It was Dr Chandrasi's sombre voice.But first tell me, what prompted a young computer engineer to choose journalism?"

"Ma'am, I believe that the platform of journalism has the power to change the world for good. Shortly after my B. Tech from the prestigious GBH College, I got drawn into the world of journalism. It was an internship to begin with, but my technical skills soon drew the attention of my seniors. My research papers in international journals led to this famous media house, where I got the opportunity to learn the nuances under the guidance of the best hands in the industry."

"Hmm, it is good to see youngsters in journalism," said Dr Chandrasi. "Did you find anything unusual about the passengers yesterday aboard UV 432?"

Kraman thought for a while, "Well, I am not sure whether this would be of help to you or not, but I did observe one suspicious person. Please have a look at this photograph. The first one was on the flight with us. I have just now found that he has two other identities." Kraman went on to describe the information recently shared with Police Officer Diganta.

Dr Chandrasi's face grimaced with anger as she shared the photo through her secure system with the NIU Chief. "That is a big lead, Chandrasi," said the Chief. "Just give me a few moments as my team is running the photos in the criminal database. Well, in the last five years, there is nothing against Viraj. Previous records are manually maintained, so it may take some time.

But wait, Viraj has been just now named as a prime suspect in the high-profile Kavya murder case. His case status is updating as we speak."

Dr Chandrasi asked Kraman to wait in the office as she proceeded towards De Silva Sir's war room. Within ten minutes, she was there and found him briskly pacing in the room. It was hot inside; perhaps the air conditioner in the room was not working properly. Then she looked at the remote. Sir had forgotten to switch on the air conditioner. He did not even notice her arrival. She switched on the remote and wished him, "Good afternoon, Sir." Hearing her voice, De Silva's tense face relaxed a bit.

"Ah, come Chandrasi, there are a lot of developments in the case. I was wondering why this Viraj, aka Lal Kunwar, doesn't have footprints in the criminal database? Police seemed to be chasing only Durjan, almost oblivious to his other identities. There is a possibility of powerful people in the system protecting Viraj. My team has zeroed in, on few suspects behind the hijack and Ransomware attacks. We have to take these threats seriously, as they could be precursors of an impending attack. Let me warn you: they seem to be plotting against you and NODO. Kavya's death is very much linked to this case," said NIU Chief De Silva.

"So Kavya got killed because she knew too much?" Chandrasi asked in an anxious tone. "Yes, the forensics team has found the happy birthday note in her house with the sender's initials as SS. He could be the same person whom Lenkesh had sent his last email."

"But what did Lenkesh and Kavya have in common? She was born in London and would have hardly been eleven or twelve years old at the time of Lenkesh's death. I don't think they ever met," said Dr Chandrasi.

De Silva Sir thought for a while and nodded his head. "See, the point that I want to make here is not about their meeting each other. What I am stressing is, that they seem to be having a common acquaintance. Someone who was a confidante of Lenkesh in 2004, and remember, he trusted this person even more than his son Atrin. That is why he chose to send the last email to this mysterious person."

Even after two decades, he remains close enough to Kavya, sends her gifts on friendiversary. And mind you, the gifts were not randomly picked. They were specially ordered for her from Malaysia.

Chandrasi, our biggest challenge is that this time, we are dealing with white-collar criminals who seemingly don't have a criminal record. The King is sitting comfortably, and it is just the pawns who are out in the open. "The hijack and ransomware attack appears to be a part of their game plan to discredit and destroy project TECHSIKA," De Silva said.

"We are pitted against heavyweights and not petty criminals. It is not about who is holding the gun, but more importantly, who has ordered the kill?" Right now, it appears like a wild maze with people of varying ideologies coming together to share a piece of cake.

At this juncture, I am not ordering action against them because I don't want to forewarn the mastermind. He is still out of our reach, hiding behind a mask. "I want you and your team to be on high alert till your press conference on the fifteenth of March. Do whatever is in your control to protect

TECHSIKA. It is our country's future and should not fall into the wrong hands."

"Since you are here, why don't you have a look at the photographs of some of the suspects?" Said Chief De Silva, "See if they have some connection with NODO." He then called his deputy and asked him to accompany Dr Chandrasi to the evidence room.

As she was looking at the photos, a commando handed over the dossier of the latest investigations about the virus attack sent by the NIU Chief.

Dr Chandrasi had not seen any of these people before at NODO. Two of them were big names, but she never had any interaction, be it personal or professional, with them. She proceeded to her car and opened the dossier; her worst fears had come true.

'It is a bioweapon to be used in biological warfare.'

The report clearly stated that the virus had no foreign origin. It was created at a local level, here itself, to inflict pain and suffering on our own people.

It had never happened before, a bioweapon being used on our soil. She was furious.

"Who are these ruthless mercenaries from our own country attacking our own people? How did they manage to masquerade themselves for so long? They are nothing but murderers, and their hands are stained with the blood of innocent villagers. They need to be exposed; their mask needs to be removed," she said forcefully.

"Now, I understand why the procurement of MNG capsules was not difficult for them. If they have the capability and infrastructure to create a virus in the lab and release it in a specific area, that means we are up against a mighty opponent. Their network is entrenched in our system like a Trojan code disguising itself as a legitimate entity. But how deep their network is? Is there a mole at NODO too?"

On her way back to the office, Dr Chandrasi could visualise her opponents moving around in the garb of bellicose sharks, waiting for her instinctive defence mechanisms to be extinguished. "I have to force the mastermind to come out in the open. This fight is not only about us but also our future generations."

She decided to hit out at her opponents with all the might of NODO, as the ticking time bomb could explode anytime.

XVI

"Well, Kraman, it seems you have ruffled feathers of the high and mighty," said Dr Chandrasi solemnly as she returned to her office. "Be careful of Viraj. He is the prime suspect in the Kavya murder case. But first, tell me what brings you here. What is the big story that you are tracking at Nabinagar?" Kraman started narrating the incidents in sequence since the previous morning. Once he finished, there was a gentle smile on her face. "So both of us were in the same boat. Or should I say flight?"

"Ma'am, I have something more to show you. I am in possession of magical sand; it seems to be having medicinal powers. Please don't laugh at me. I am telling the truth." Kraman bowed his head, fearing derision. He did not notice Dr Chandrasi's discomforted eyes watching him intently. "Can you show me that sand?" She asked.

"Yes, Ma'am." Kraman took out the envelope and handed it over to her. She did not utter a single word for a few moments as she looked inside it. Her face grew tense as a bowstring, and she closed her eyes for a moment, contemplating her next step. Then she took out a wristwatch from her bag and gave it to Kraman.

"This is for your protection. In case of any emergency, just press the SOS button on the watch. Once the button is pressed, my team will get the visual feed of the area within a hundred metres. There is a tracker inside the phone. In case the watch is forcibly removed from your wrist, my team will get a notification. My number is saved as Secret Santa, but you cannot make or receive calls to any other number through this watch. You can only call Secret Santa."

Just then, there was a call from Diganta.

"Be careful," she said as Kraman sought her leave to go back to the hospital.

Firstly hijack, then the Ransomware attack, and now this mysterious sand. "Double the security of our main lab," she instructed her secretary.

"AMBAK- the EYE will have to be activated soon. I can't take a chance," said Dr Chandrasi as she moved towards the Zeta Con to set the perimeter alert for activation. The security of TECHSIKA was supreme, and only AMBAK- the EYE could ensure that.

Soon, the area around TECHSIKA would become secure. No machines, no divers, no submersibles, nothing could go near it for the next forty-eight hours. That was the safe time limit wherein the activation of AMBAK-the EYE had no adverse effect on the aquatic ecosystem. At NODO, maintaining the ecological balance has always been a non-negotiable policy.

The exact coordinates were to be sent to NAVY after confirmation by the eleven o'clock underwater mission team on the fifteenth of March. The sea bed and its treasures do have a drifting tendency. As a seasoned marine biologist, Dr Chandrasi knew it well.

The plan suited her as it provided a breather to identify the saboteur within. Although it was hard for her to believe that someone from NODO was in cahoots with the enemy, the fact remained that critical information was being leaked. Who else but an insider could have access to all this data?

Kraman was dropped at the hospital gate by NODO's driver. "How is Kaka? I hope he is better now," said Kraman. A distressed Diganta got up from the chair, embraced him, and continued crying inconsolably. "There is no improvement in Kaka's condition. I just now spoke to the doctor; he is still critical."

They stood silently for a few minutes, praying to the Almighty for a miracle.

The waiting area will be closed for the next thirty minutes, the message flashed on the big screen. "I think it is the drill," said Diganta. Tomorrow, there is going to be a packed house at the Rainbow Conclave, plus so many VIPs are expected. The hospital needs to gear up for any eventuality. The administration can take no chances. Let's wait outside.

That very moment,he received a wireless message.

"I have to go to the police station. There seems to be an emergency, said Diganta. You wait outside or else go to the guesthouse and get some rest. Doctors have told me to come after two hours."

As Diganta turned round the corner, Kraman's phone rang. It was an unknown number. Within a minute, there was a message from the same number. 'Call me if you want to know about Kavya.'

"Who could this be?" Kraman thought while climbing the stairs near the exit. The journalist in him soon took over, and he dialled the last number. There was a gruff voice on the other side, "I can tell you why Kavya was killed."

Kraman decided to take the bait and mocked the caller, "So you are pretending to be Sanjay from Mahabharata, relaying to me the incidents of the fateful night! But mind you, I am no Dhritrashtra. I can see well through your concocted story."

Well, the mysterious caller paused. "You are indeed right. I was watching her room live on the night of the twelfth of March. Actually, we had sent the pest control team to Kavya's house a week ago and had a bug planted in her laptop. Whenever the laptop was switched on, it activated the recording mode. We could see everything that happened in the front of the laptop. Don't take me wrong," said the caller. "We were forced to do this; rather, she brought it upon herself. Since her induction as a majority stakeholder in PENAK Associates, she has been sticking her nose everywhere, particularly in SP's dealings."

"So, you are telling me that SP got her killed?" Kraman's voice was quivering with angst. The caller was a bit reticent and then spoke decisively.

"SP did not order the hit on Kavya. He had nothing to do with it. She was Mamak's daughter's best friend. Everyone knows that Mamak loves his daughter, and any attempt on her best friend would be construed as a direct attack on Mamak. Do you think SP is so naive to have a direct confrontation with Mamak and risk all his business ties?"

You have played so much football, Kraman and yet your conjectures are so offside. I thought you knew that one needs to follow the rules for scoring the goal.

So, the caller knows about my passion for football. It was not a random call! "But why should I believe you?" Kraman shouted. "I need to see Kavya's laptop and her iPhone. And by the way, how the hell are you in possession of her laptop and mobile? But before that, who are you, and why are you telling me all this? Are you pretending to be a saviour?"

"Hold your horses, Kraman and pause for a bit. Remember your article in the college magazine about the sand mafia, which won the Golden Letter Award at the national level and was published in all the leading newspapers?" It was your Greta Thunberg moment. So, yes, we do have an association. You had written so much against us as if we were monsters. But tell me, with so much sand around us, what harm was it if we had taken a fistful?

Coming to your volley of questions, two of my men climbed through the pipes to enter Kavya's room. We had seen that her window was open. My men picked up her laptop, mobile, and the gifts received that evening. They locked the door of the bedroom from the inside and again came down the pipes from the window.

And now, let me introduce myself. "I am Viraj. I'm sending the last video file on Kavya's laptop as proof of our presence in her room. Ah! More recently, let me brush your memory; we flew together on flight UV 432 as co-passengers. I am sending Kavya's laptop and iPhone to Dr Chandrasi. As we speak, the packet has been delivered to her."

"Do you really believe that a top scientist would interact with a shady person like you, Viraj? Someone who has been named as a prime suspect in Kavya's murder case? I think you are scared as investigations have begun against you," Kraman turned aggressive as he saw that Viraj was trying to play mind games with him.

You are quite sharp, Kraman. But let me update you, "I sent a photograph to Dr Chandrasi, and seeing the powerful people in the photo, she called me immediately and we are meeting tomorrow at the closing ceremony of Rainbow City." The phone disconnected with a click.

Just then, he received a video on his WhatsApp number. It was sent by the last caller, claiming to be Viraj. Was he really speaking the truth? Was it really the recording of the final moments of Kavya? How could someone be so inhuman to record her last gasps and show it as a trophy? Kraman opened the video file with trembling hands.

It was six fifteen in the evening when the maid entered Kavya's room and kept the gift box and bouquet of flowers near her bed. "Madam, I will be back in a moment with your aam panna[39]."

"Mayuri must have sent these gifts for our friendiversary ," said Kavya excitedly as she proceeded to open her gift. "Where are the scissors," said Kavya as she looked admiringly at the artistically packed gift box. She opened her bedside drawer and found a pocket knife instead. But her expression changed from curiosity to shock as she took off the gift wrap.

---

[39] *raw mango drink*

Her face turned pale, and she froze. The pocket knife fell from her hand and hit the floor. She stood like a statue and did not move for a while. She raised her left hand in defence and fell on the bed with a thud. Then came the powerful hiss sound. The deadly Saw-Scaled Viper and Blue Malaysian Coral snake sprang their heads. They had been inside the box for quite some time and leapt at the instant the cover was removed. It all happened in a flash. The slender serpents slithered silently, their scaly skins shimmering in the LED lights as their tongues occasionally flicked out to taste the fear in the surroundings.

Just then, the door opened, and the maid entered with a glass of juice. She kept it on the window. Then, looking at the skies, she asked, "Why don't you call Mayuri Madam here only? The skies look overcast, and it might rain heavily. I will make your favourite rasgullas at home."

Getting no response, she turned back and spotted the dangerous snakes moving towards her. Sensing no way forward, the maid jumped out of the window. That was the last shot on the video file.

Kraman's hands were shaking like a leaf as he tried to hold the mobile. Use of poisonous snakes as a murder weapon, he could not believe his own eyes. The sender must have sent two deadly snakes on purpose to petrify Kavya. He wanted to kill her by shock and hence the crime scene was staged to look like a suicide, with her room locked from the inside.

Such a brutal end for someone as humane and gentle as Kavya! It took him a while to recompose himself as he sat under a nearby tree.

NODO was on high alert.All the staff members had been informed about the security drill and were told to switch off their phones till the next instruction. CCTVs began relaying the pictures of the staff members working at their workstations. Dr Chandrasi was herself, monitoring the feed as it went to the AI (artificial intelligence) enabled machine, which analysed the facial expressions of the staff in real-time mode. Wherever it observed any kind of discomfort or lack of concentration, it was programmed to send an alert to the main server.

Half an hour had elapsed when the first alert was sounded by the machine's face analytics software. There were three faces on Dr Chandrasi's monitor. The first one had been on a month's leave for an important surgery and had joined the office today itself. He still had difficulty in sitting continuously in the same posture and was changing his chair position frequently. But it was the second and the third face that unsettled her. Surti and Sanya, how was it possible? Both of them had been in NODO for almost two decades.

She prompted the machine for the smartwatch data on their wrists. These watches provided by NODO were meant to keep a tab on their health. The employees had agreed to share their data in emergencies. Pulse rates, as well as the heartbeats of Surti and Sanya, were irregular. She checked it with the previous month's data; their vital signs had always been in normal range. She grew suspicious and decided to probe further.

She looked for their personal details on the computer. Surti joined NODO in 2002, and Sanya joined a year later. Both had worked at Lalpura under Lenkesh. Their CR

(Confidential Reports) had either Excellent or Very Good ratings.Even the personal files had no adverse comments.

It was then, she called De Silva Sir and requested him to check these names. Meanwhile, the face analytics software did not show any fresh alerts. She called her secretary to get two promotion orders ready, one in the name of Surti and another for Sanya. After she signed them, the orders were faxed to Lalpura and delivered to Surti and Sanya.

"Well, I have found these names in the economic offender's list," said De Silva. "Mr Surti and Miss Sanya got their marriage registered in November 2004, and you would be surprised to know that Lenkesh had been a witness to their marriage. The couple has been gifted a couple of plum properties in posh locations by Atrin."

"But why did they keep their marriage a secret? No one at NODO knows that they are a couple. All these years, they pretended to be colleagues, but why? Our organisation wholeheartedly embraces people irrespective of their backgrounds," said Dr Chandrasi.

"It could be their strategy to circumvent any suspicion," said De Silva. "In case one's cover got blown, the other could continue spying. I will send my men to pick them up for interrogation."

"Oh no, Sir, that might alarm the mastermind. Let Surti and Sanya enjoy their promotion order for a day at least." De Silva was taken aback by this news. "What! You have promoted them?"

"Sir, what other option did I have to track them? My trusted Deputy at the Lalpura office sprayed the bug chemical (as we call it) on the promotion order before delivering it to them. As they received the order, the chemical instantly spread to their palms. So, for the next forty-eight hours, we can track their physical activity. This chemical cannot be detected by any anti-bugging device. This promotion elevates Surti to the post of Incharge of the special diver suits section and Sanya, as the deputy head of our research wing.

"You mean the special suit which enables a diver to go underwater even when AMBAK-the EYE has been activated?" De Silva was clearly at a loss for words. "But we all know how important the suit is for our underwater missions. And particularly at this juncture, putting TECHSIKA at stake? I don't understand Chandrasi," he said in a startled tone.

He closed his eyes for a few seconds and tapped his head. Thereafter, he took out his spectacle and looked at her, and both started smilingly. "Ah, I get it; the ferromagnetic sole in the diver gear. You should work with us," said De Silva."This plan of yours sounds more like an investigator than a scientist! Elevating Surti and Sanya to sensitive posts would make them believe that they are orchestrating the plot well. In their overconfidence, they will make a careless move, and then we will catch them red-handed. That will also expose the mastermind behind this."

"Although I hate to admit Sir, but this is the first time that I wish to be proven wrong. My own people are working against the national interest; it is a disgrace! But here at NODO, we follow the rule of law, and if Surti and Sanya are guilty, then they will be dealt with accordingly. After two hours, a special consignment of four special diver suits will move out from our production facility. Surti does not know that all of them have been retrofitted with ferromagnetic soles. As Incharge, he has the final say on the quality and number of suits. If less than four suits are cleared by him, then he is our man."

It was a notification on Kraman's mobile, which brought a smile to his face. His favourite Team Pikachu, the masters at nail-biting finishes and high-voltage octane drama, had won the DOTA state championship. And finally, the much-awaited announcement of E-sports debuting as a medal sport at the upcoming Continental Games had been made. Kraman was happy but not in celebration mode today. He was worried about Suyash Kaka's health. There was so much at stake.

"I must go inside and speak to the doctor on duty," thought Kraman as he moved towards the hospital gate. "Diganta seems to be stuck up at the police station. The waiting area must have opened by now." Suddenly, a police van screeched to a halt on his right side, and he was pulled in. The chloroform did the rest. Kraman's head was hazy as he gained semi-consciousness about twenty minutes later. He could see four men in the van, including the driver.

"Welcome, Kraman," it was Viraj on the video call. "You were looking for my photo and bank accounts.Save the trouble, here I am, live in action!" Actually, I bluffed when I told you that a meeting had been fixed with Dr Chandrasi. That was my plan A, but I could not contact her in the first instance. So, I sent Kavya's last moment's clip to gain your trust. You are nothing but my plan B.

But now I have received personal confirmation from Dr Chandrasi. I don't need you anymore. It is my city, my rules.

Your article created trouble for us, and now is the time to settle the score.

"By the way, are you searching for the cut mark on my forehead? Well, cosmetic surgery is the name of the game," said Viraj with a wink. "And yes, don't get any false hopes that someone will report about you. You have been picked up by the police van, and for your information, the CCTV on the hospital gates is not working."

Incidentally, I am also known as Lal Kunwar, an angel investor. Yesterday, I was there at the Moksha Hotel to get the sample back from you. My eyes have been on you, both of them. Thanks to medical science, I am no more the one-eyed Durjan!

"The magical sand belonged to me, and yet you stashed it somewhere. Was that the right thing to do, Kraman? Do you have any idea about its price? My international clients are ready to pay millions for it. They call it a mystical substance. Had I been successful in retrieving the sand at Moksha, you could have easily enjoyed the grand function at Rainbow Conclave. But you chose to poke your nose into SS's affairs, so be ready to pay the price."

Kraman's hands were tied behind his back. He could not reach the SOS button on his wristwatch. The car ahead of them screeched to a halt, and his van driver also had to apply sudden brakes. Kraman fell from the seat due to the impact. The other two kidnappers helped him to get back to his seat. Little did they know that the SOS button got pressed in this struggle, and help was on the way!

"Goodbye Kraman," said Viraj. "I have to prepare for my meeting with Dr Chandrasi." Then, turning towards the driver, he said, "Call me in five minutes once you reach the old Loka - Nabinagar highway."

The driver looked in his rearview mirror. There were no vehicles on the road. He slowed a bit to check if someone was trailing them. But there was no movement, not even the usual shepherds with their herd of cattle. The old highway was in sight now as he called Viraj to confirm that the plan was on track.

As the driver stepped up the accelerator, he saw the nails and screws scattered on the road ahead. He immediately applied the brakes and alerted others in the van. "Put this young man in the dickey, and let's check for ourselves," said the driver as all of them took out their pistols and came out in a formation.They heaved a sigh of relief as the tyres looked good.

"There is a shortcut to the highway. We will take that." "Are you sure?" Asked one of the kidnappers. "Oh yes, I had taken that route a few months ago; it is just after that clearing," said the driver. They decided to check the clearing on the left side of the road, which was about two hundred metres from the position of the van.

"Should one of us wait near the van?" Asked one of them.

"But he is in the dickey, all tied up. Where will he go? Moreover, we might need hands at the clearing in case the path is blocked," said the driver.

"Let's check it fast. I have already confirmed to Viraj that we are on the highway, and you know he does not like delays."

The driver was right. Punctuality was an asset of Viraj! He had activated the timer at ten minutes after getting confirmation from the driver. The kidnappers returned to the van within four to five minutes and checked the lock on the dickey. Everything looked good, and they took the shortcut. As the van reached the old highway, there was a blast, and a notification blinked on Viraj's device: 'Mission successful, all eliminated.'

Viraj had disclosed only a part of the plan to the driver and had paid him handsomely to eliminate the journalist. This was a lesson he had learnt from his master — Neither disclose the whole plan nor leave any evidence. After all, the driver and his accomplices had become a liability, and their riddance ensured that there were no witnesses to this accident.

Durjan, aka Viraj, the once dreaded mafia don, was pushed to a corner and forced to play second fiddle to his master, who preferred to remain anonymous. By setting up a meeting with Dr Chandrasi at Rainbow Conclave, he planned to finish the story of his irritating master, who treated him like a doormat.

After that, he planned to have a fifty-fifty partnership with Atrin. His previous association with Lenkesh in ocean bed explorations had initially led to this friendship with Atrin. Rather, it was Viraj who broke the news about the failure of Lenkesh's dream project in December 2004.

"It wasn't a freak accident which killed your father," Viraj told Atrin, "It was literally a well-planned execution by NODO officials,particularly Dr Chandrasi.She didn't think twice, before acting against Lenkesh, who was one of their own. You must retaliate and avenge your father's death."

Viraj knew that he had hit the Achilles heel of Atrin, and piggybacking on this angst, he soon leapfrogged as a close confidante. Although the duo differed on their objectives, Atrin was seeking revenge, whereas Viraj was merely interested in the wealth of the ocean. But one thing was common; both considered NODO as their enemy number one.

Atrin held NODO responsible for his father's public humiliation, whereas Viraj had lost the majority of his sand business due to environmental surveys and reports of the scientists at NODO.

"I should be on time," said Viraj. "It is not good to keep the Chief Scientist of NODO waiting. I am going to reveal all the secrets of my boss to her and seek my freedom in exchange. After all, he keeps the lion's share of our profits and hence deserves the proportionate punishments, too!"

'What goes around comes around. Life is nothing but a merry-go-round.'

XVII

Meanwhile, Kraman was enjoying vada pav with the special ops commandos at the NODO office. "Kudos to your calmness in the van; the kidnappers did believe that they were in control of the situation. They went ahead with their plan confidently and never took you as a threat. The drones were keeping an eye on you once the SOS button was activated. And we were following you, albeit from a distance. We could have taken you out earlier also, but Dr Chandrasi did not want to tip off Viraj before their meeting at Rainbow Conclave."

"Yes, Viraj could be the leading man in this jigsaw puzzle, and we need to make him speak. But I must say that your team was superb. You arrived in superbikes without a sound, picked me up, and all of us vanished into thin air. The whole operation took less than three minutes," said Kraman with a big smile on his face.

"Actually the old highway is the only exit from the town, which does not have a permanent police picket. As your kidnappers moved towards it, the nails and screws were spread on the road by our team. We silently waited there on our superbikes as we knew that they would be forced to check out the shortcut, and that gave us time to execute our rescue plan," said one of the commandos.

Just then, Dr Chandrasi arrived and said, "Good to see you safe, Kraman." She thanked the commandos profusely for their Secret Santa performance. Soon, they took leave of her, and now Kraman was alone in the room with Dr Chandrasi.

"You must be wondering what brings the Chief Scientist of NODO and the NIU Chief together at Nabinagar and Loka. Certainly, we are not here to attend this function at Rainbow Conclave! Actually, I should have told you about the magical sand earlier.

We had reports of a virus outbreak in the Sona Ghaati. This onset of virus infection coinciding with the planning of the Rainbow City project seemed unusual to us. You might have read in the newspapers that initially, the people were not ready to relocate; in fact, they are still protesting."

"Oh, so this virus attack is being used to scare the people so that they move out of Sona Ghaati," said an alarmed Kraman.

"Now, this sudden virus outbreak, whether it has a natural origin or was it developed in a lab, it is a classified investigation. The National Intelligence Unit Chief is pursuing the case." But the people are suffering a lot due to this virus attack. You would have observed many people here wearing full shirts, caps or shawls, even in this hot and humid weather. Actually, these people are infected by the virus and are trying to hide their symptoms.

"But the good news is that NODO's research wing has developed the perfect combination for its cure. The latest clinical trial results indicate that it is going to be a boon for the virus-infected patients. The core ingredient of this new drug is the super sand-like material from our ocean, and it has magical healing properties. See, it looks like sand but is denser and heavier. This is what you received in the envelope also," said Dr Chandrasi. "A layman might confuse the processed material with sand, but they are entirely different. The naturally occurring molecules in this wonderful source material are like Samudra Dev[40]'s blessings." Believe me, it is bound to trigger a revolution in the medical world.

But somehow, this news got leaked, and our main production facility at Angira was attacked. Although the intruders could not access the main lab and were killed in the counterfiring, one of the small packets of processed sand which was ready for dispatch went missing after the incident. The production facility Incharge presumed it to be lost in the melee of gunshots and did not put it in his final report.

I came to know of it when you showed the sand to me. An enquiry has been initiated against the production facility Incharge of Angira. "But thanks to you, now we know for sure that Viraj was behind the attack at our production facility. You put your life on the line for the country, young man! I am so proud of you. Now go and have some rest," said Dr Chandrasi, patting Kraman.

"I am good, madam. I will go and see if Suyash Kaka's health has improved," said Kraman. "My driver will drop you at the hospital," said Dr Chandrasi, "Ah! In case you need help in Suyash's case, I suggest you share the evidence with De Silva Sir. I owe you one big time," she said dialling the National Investigative Unit (NIU) Chief's number.

Now it was Chief De Silva's turn to get startled. "How do you know Kraman? Is his kidnapping connected to this

---

[40] *Ocean God*

case?" "Yes, sir, Viraj considered him a threat, and that is why he tried to eliminate him. I have a hunch that Kraman has been attacked due to his proximity to Suyash. Actually, Suyash and SP's enmity is more than two decades old," said Dr Chandrasi, "Kraman had told me that Suyash was jailed because of SP."

"So are you saying that SP sent Viraj to eliminate this journalist, Kraman? If it is so, then we have a solid case against SP. He is already number one on my suspects' list," said De Silva. "But we are dealing with a sensitive national matter. Would it be okay to involve Kraman?"

Dr Chandrasi briefly narrated about his being invited to Rainbow City by Suyash and the attempted theft of the processed sand material. "Sir, he is the one who brought Viraj's multiple identities to our notice."

"Okay, Chandrasi, I will speak to him. If Suyash's accusations are true, I will ensure that he gets justice. The time has come for SP to realise that no man is above the law."

As Kraman got down at the hospital's gate, the phone alarm rang in Kraman's pocket. There were two missed calls by Nancy from Rainbow Conclave. The function was to start in half an hour. He moved towards the Intensive Care Unit, where Diganta was pacing in the corridor. The crestfallen look on his face indicated that there wasn't any improvement in Kaka's health.

"Years of incarceration and melancholy has taken a toll on his body.He has slipped into a coma," said the doctor. Kraman and Diganta tried holding the railing as their feet seemingly refused to hold their body weight. They held hands together, praying for Suyash Kaka.

"A man in his prime youth lost Kali Babu, a fatherly figure and Suchita, his childhood friend and fiancée. His own family severed relations with him, and he was socially outcast. His name and reputation were charred beyond recognition as his life was wasted in prison. Come what may,his name needs to be cleared," said Diganta. Both knew the importance of nabbing the real culprit and absolving Suyash Kaka from the crimes he never committed.

"I am not going to the inauguration function at Rainbow Conclave. I will wait at the hospital." But Diganta, I don't understand why Viraj is coming to meet Dr Chandrasi at the Rainbow Conclave?

"Maybe his own life is in danger, and he has chosen this crowded venue for his own safety," said Diganta. "He knows that he is the prime suspect in the Kavya murder case, and his bosses would love to offload him."

"I think you should know this incident about Durjan. Suyash Kaka had met one sand mafia Qala in prison. He was supposedly the right-hand man of Durjan, and it was rumoured that he was being pressurised to turn approver in the sand mafia case. One night, he was brutally attacked inside the jail and had to be hospitalised. Due to his low blood pressure, Suyash Kaka was also at the hospital. Both of them were allotted adjacent beds for the next two nights in the special jail ward.

It was the second night when Qala told Suyash Kaka that he works for Durjan."Initially, he was the boss, but over the years, I observed that Durjan ceded power to someone else. No one in the group was aware of the identity of their new boss. Durjan took orders from him and got them executed through people like me."

Their group was no longer the sand mafia of Niskashi alone; they had mushroomed to a wider geography. Now, they had labs and docking stations near the ocean. Qala had never been inside them but had seen foreigners entering the labs many times.

And most importantly, he said, lowering his voice, "Durjan donned a new identity as police declared him a fugitive. He went underground for some time, and a big bounty was put on his head. In his new identity, he was hardly recognisable."

Suddenly, at that moment, the doctor came on rounds. He checked on Qala and called for the nurse to shift him to the ICU immediately as his blood pressure was falling rapidly. The next morning, Suyash Kaka was sent back to prison, and almost a month later, he was released. He did not get a chance to see Qala again."

"Did Qala speak about Durjan's new business?" Asked Kraman impatiently. "No, Kaka told me that the doctor's sudden arrival silenced Qala. He was on the cusp of revealing something, but the sound of the door cut short their conversation."

But last month, a young man came looking for Suyash Kaka with a small packet. He was Qala's youngest son. He said, "My father had told me to give this packet to you in case something happens to him." "What happened to Qala? Is he still in jail?" Suyash Kaka asked in an agitated tone.

"Well, he had agreed to be an approver in the case. He was being taken in the police van to the court when the van overturned and caught fire. The policemen jumped out of the vehicle, but my father and two other prisoners got trapped inside and were burnt alive," said Qala's son in a choking voice.

Alarmed by this incident, Suyash Kaka asked me to arrange an invitation to Rainbow Conclave in your name. Then he took out an old-looking envelope and touched it time and again with tenderness. His eyes were misty as he told me to arrange to and fro flight tickets and a room reservation at Hotel Moksha for you. By the way, how was your stay at the hotel? I had booked a normal room, but they upgraded you under some scheme."

"Yes, the room was superb. It made me assume that my sponsor is an affluent person. But now you are telling me that I just got lucky!" Kraman's funny side made Diganta smile, and it eased the atmosphere a bit.

"When I returned," Diganta continued, "the contents of the packet were lying on the table. There was some sand-like material, and a few lines scribbled on a piece of paper. I was surprised; did Qala lose his life just for this ?

Kaka gave me the piece of paper and asked me to copy it on the backside of the invitation letter in invisible ink. Then he told me to add the last two lines of the riddle, asking you to meet him at gate number seven on the thirteenth of March. Thereafter, he asked me to burn the paper. I got that envelope delivered to your flat through one of my men.

"Thanks Diganta, for providing the missing link in this puzzle. So Qala was Kaka's informer, and that is why he had all the information. The riddle was formed by Qala in the prison. Even if the jail authorities seized the piece of paper, it would not have been easy for them to decipher the riddle. I think Qala's son is going to be of help in the investigation against SP."

"But SP is too powerful and might try to eliminate him just like his father. He needs police protection. I will arrange for it," said Diganta. "His testimony against SP is going to be crucial in this case."

"But first let's go and see Kaka, his condition is still very critical," said Diganta as both moved towards the ICU, hoping for some good news.

Meanwhile, Dr Chandrasi had reached the closing ceremony alone, without any official entourage. As expected, the crowd was boisterous. Bigwigs and hotshots from politics, Bollywood and business fraternity had descended at the venue. The entry of two IPL stars added to the crowd's adrenaline. Arrangements by PENAK Associates looked great! The huge crowd was merrily foot-tapping on Bollywood numbers.

The crowd was not moving like pebbles in a jar. Rather, they looked like water molecules flowing smoothly past one another. The ambience at the Conclave transported her to the good old college days.

But her eyes were looking for Viraj as she checked her watch again. Ah, there he is! She signalled to the vacant seat beside her. Viraj nodded his head and settled in the chair while thrusting a paper in her hands. Before she could open it, the skies were lit up with bright lights. The crowd was gazing in awe at the massive fireworks display. Some shooting stars went straight up, a few whirled in a spiral, some shattered into thousands of fabulous sparks, and others seemed floating in a dazzling blizzard.

No one noticed the shots being fired at point-blank range with the silencer gun. The shots were clean, and the target was instantly down. The National Anthem started playing in the background. All stood up except one.

Chandrasi looked at Viraj, sitting motionless on his chair. The bullets had pierced his heart. His face was terror-stricken as if he had seen a ghost. It appeared from the look on his face that he knew the shooter but was not expecting him to be here. The shooter was a gatecrasher, but he was a pro for sure. The work was absolutely clean; no helter-skelter.

Stepping back from her seat, she clicked on the tiny yellow button on her spectacles. The emergency teams at NODO now had her precise location. They could see the area around her through the tiny cameras on the spectacle. The precincts were soon secured by the Rescue team of NODO. She swiftly moved to the back gate, where a bullet proof car was waiting for her.

Code Omega had been activated twice in two days, once at the Airport and now at the Conclave. Chandrasi's mind was busy deciphering whether Viraj was the target or he paid the price of being there with her. She looked at the paper thrust in her hand by Viraj. It was scribbled hastily – 'You are in danger. Beware of Shark Kothi.' On the back of it was a snake with its tail in the mouth. The drawing was not very clear, but it did look like the symbol of Ouroboros.

"One thing was sure: Viraj had access to important information. And that is why someone wanted to eliminate him before he passed on the information to me," thought Chandrasi, "But he had all the time on the flight. He could have easily spoken to me. What made him flip in twenty-four hours from non-cooperation to cooperation? Why this change of heart?"

"Track all the physical movements and call records of Viraj for the last forty-eight hours ASAP," she directed her bodyguard, Navjeet, sitting in the front seat of the car. "NIU Chief is on his way to our office, Ma'am. He is a bit cross with you for moving without security."

"I know that going alone to the Conclave was a bit of a rash decision. Please inform him that I am absolutely safe," said Dr Chandrasi. "By the way did our Rescue team nab the shooter?" "Not yet, Ma'am. He seems to have merged with the crowd. Our team is checking the CCTV as well as drone camera footage for any suspicious activity. But till now, we don't have a single shot of the person who fired at Viraj."

Chandrasi knew the essence of time in this case. As the clock was ticking, the shooter was drifting away from them. Viraj was the link between various players in this dangerous game. His death ensured the extension of the picture-perfect good citizen image of his partners. And that is why she was angry with herself. She had lost a chance today to unmask the veiled siphoners of public money.

"Ma'am, our team has just updated that Viraj had two mobiles in his pocket. One had about thirty-eight calls, but all were regular calls. Nothing suspicious has been found so far.

The team is calling all the numbers to confirm their alibi. But his other phone has been used only thrice in the last forty-eight hours. The first one is, of course, your official number Ma'am.

Interestingly, he received a call from an unknown number, and immediately, he dialled a journalist named Kraman. So it seems that this unknown caller told him something so important that Viraj needed to contact the journalist."

The NIU Chief was pacing briskly till her car reached the war room at NODO. "Good to see you, Chandrasi," he said in a concerned tone as she entered the room. "You are a good biologist, one of the best I have seen. But a bit impulsive at times. Next time you move without security, I am going to report it for sure."

"Next time, it won't happen, De Silva Sir." She said with an apologetic face, which seemed to relax him. "Come what may, tomorrow, the project will be unveiled as per schedule. A commitment is a commitment!" Declared Chandrasi. Her eyes brimmed with pride as the Chief raised his hand for the high five. Just then, Navjeet knocked on the door. "Kraman's location is near the hospital, Ma'am. Should we send a team to pick him up?"

"Oh no, I have already sent him a message. He should be here anytime. He had received a riddle from Suyash that might give us some more clues. Tomorrow is our big day, and we must put our best foot forward. Let's not leave anything to chance."

Kraman arrived in about ten minutes with the invitation letter in his hand. After Viraj's murder, the riddle was their lifeline now. "The first two lines refer to the Nabinagar triad of SP, Mamak and Lenkesh," said NIU Chief De Silva Sir. "And after Lenkesh's death, the threesome SP, Mamak and Atrin took control. I am sure about the riddle referring to these three, as their names have come up multiple times in our investigation. Currently, these three are at the top of our list of suspects. Their association runs deep, and they have been together through thick and thin. The easy availability of henchmen like Viraj on their roll call have strengthened their crime syndicate."

"Yes. Viraj's involvement in this murky business is established without doubt. Once he realised he was being cornered by the police authorities, he tried to play the role of a good samaritan by divulging information about his partners. But that is not going to absolve him of his criminal antecedents and all the wrongdoings," the NIU Chief thundered.

"The queen in the riddle is Dr Chandrasi and it refers to the recent attacks on her life," said De Silva loudly. "And the people behind all this mayhem are not new; they are your old enemies, Chandrasi. Perhaps old wine in a new bottle refers to that. It is definitely the fight for control of the ocean's wealth."

"The riddle is almost solved. But what could be the meaning of Shark Kothi turning green? Has it been used figuratively?" Chandrasi spoke aloud as she took out the last note of Viraj, 'Beware of Shark Kothi', and showed it to the Chief. It is used twice, once in Qala's riddle and then in Viraj's note.

"I have a hunch that it is a place inside the forest, maybe so deep in the dense forest that the colour of the place merges with the greenery around," said Kraman. "And this symbol on Viraj's note does look like Ouroboros (a circular symbol depicting a snake swallowing its own tail. As an emblem of infinity, it represents the eternal cycle of destruction and recreation)."

"I agree with Kraman," said Dr Chandrasi as she took out the photo that Viraj had sent her yesterday along with Kavya's laptop and iPhone. "It was this photo that prompted me to meet him alone at the Rainbow Conclave."

Everyone in the room drew close to the table to see the picture. There were four men - SP, Mamak, Atrin and Viraj standing with the Gold of Kinabalu orchid painting forming a beautiful background. On the back side of the picture,there was the initials - 'SS' (pic courtesy).

Just then, the intercom buzzed. It was her IT expert. "Ma'am, the location of Viraj's last caller has been triangulated. It is in a dense forest. We will have to manually search in a radius of about eight to nine hundred metres. We are sending our night drones for precise location, but the mobile network seems to be very poor in the area."

The NIU Chief agreed that the forest area was not safe at night. "I will be sending an advance party in the morning at five am, and Kraman will accompany us fifteen minutes later. And Chandrasi, I know you wish to come along, but it would be better if you stay here in the war room and watch it live from within the safe precincts." The NIU Chief's voice was almost like a command.

"Dr Chandrasi speaks highly about you," said the NIU Chief,

turning towards Kraman as they both moved out of the room. "Sir, I have something very important to show you, which could have an important bearing on our case," said Kraman as he submitted the file against SP. Dummy transactions, fictitious entries and, above all, mala fide intent adding to the web of termites gobbling the Kali Industries.

"Sir, you might not find SP's fingerprints on the trigger, but Kali Babu's life was lost because of him. He not only overtook the business empire surreptitiously but also demolished the values and morals which were close to Kali Babu's heart. He snatched everything from Suyash Kaka and ruined his life; maybe it was the price for trusting an unreliable man like SP!

How can I forget that SP destroyed Suchita didi's life, which was in no way connected to his skulduggery?" Asked Kraman in a voice choked with emotion. "She was like a civilian caught in a crossfire and missing in action.I have not seen her since that day in Chandinagar."

"Chandrasi had spoken to me about this. It sounds like a water-tight case against SP," said Chief solemnly after going through the papers. "Putting him behind bars may sound herculean , but don't worry. I am putting my best men on this job as we speak. How is Suyash? Can we count him as a witness? No, sir, he is in a coma, and there are slim chances of recovery. But there is Qala's son who is willing to testify against SP in the court."

"That is great, young man. Now go and have some rest. There is pretty action coming up tomorrow," said Chief in his authoritarian voice.

"And one thing more, I am taking you tomorrow with me as an expert since you know a lot about this case. But don't forget that you are a civilian and must stay behind the lines and listen to my men. We are on a dangerous mission, and my men will not hesitate to use firepower if the condition arises. In such a case as an unarmed individual, don't attempt any heroics. My men are trained to handle such situations. I hope I am clear," said NIU Chief.

"Yes sir," said Kraman as they moved to their respective rooms. "Good night, sir. Let's meet early in the morning."

Kraman was tossing and turning in the bed, unable to settle down for the night. Whether he was distraught by today's happenings, or was it his own quest for closure? He was unsure as darkness engulfed the room, and the clouds hid the moon for a few minutes. Kraman closed his eyes as memories of his childhood began to flash by.

Isn't it a sentimental journey to relive the passions of the past, reminiscing one's hopes and fears? But for Kraman, it entailed a lot of pain as he harked back to the good old days with Suchita didi at Chandinagar. Their families lived close by, and incidentally, their journey began together from the famous St. Mary's School .

It was her first day as a teacher and for Kraman, it was first day as a student of baby pre-nursery. Both looked nervous and clasped each other's hands as they walked inside the school gate. Their bonding and friendship grew over the years. Of course, the Vada pav in Suchita's tiffin increased as Kraman cutely asked every morning, "What have you got in tiffin, didi?". His innocent eyes and cute smile prompted Suchita to bring two tiffins.

She was a gifted storyteller who could spin amusing tales from everyday life. Every morning she had a new story on the way to school.Kraman was so enticed by her stories that he never missed a single day of school and had a hundred percent attendance!

One day, he saw her house being decorated for marriage and was so happy. Celebrations and festivities were in the air as guests began arriving at her house in Chandinagar.

Then something happened. Suchita didi stopped coming to school. The decorations and lights around her house were removed. The beautiful Shaadi Pandal[41] was dismantled. One day she left Chandinagar abruptly and Kraman cried a lot, the pain in his heart was too much to bear.He waited for her every morning, but never saw her again. Since that day, he never celebrated Rakshabandhan!

One of the tragedies in life is that no amount of wealth is enough to buy a ticket to our past. The bygone days are done and dusted; one cannot relive the past. But is it easy to take a call on the tussle between hanging on and letting go?

With the NIU Chief's backing, he was sure that Suyash Kaka would get justice. He sneaked into the night and took an auto rickshaw to the hospital. Kaka was still in coma. The kind-hearted nurse allowed him inside the ICU for just two minutes to see Kaka. Kraman's eyes were misty as he held Kaka's hands and promised, "SP is going to pay for the sins he committed against you and Suchita didi. I know you

---

[41] *temporarily erected structure where marriage was to be solemnised*

waited for a long time for justice, but there is going to be no more delay. SP will be behind bars soon."

"Did he really grasp my hand, or was it my imagination?" thought Kraman. The nurse was coming towards him. He knew it was time to go. He touched Kaka's feet one last time and left the hospital.

Around four a.m., there was a call from the hospital. "Suyash opened his eyes around half an hour earlier," said the doctor, "In his feeble voice, he called your name, and then he called Suchita. His face looked so fresh. I have been treating him for the last few months, but never saw this level of contentment. The nurse told me you were with him late at night. Whatever you said, it made him happy."

"How is he now?" Asked Kraman.

"He passed away at 3.45am. It seems he was just waiting for your golden words. It gave him peace and closure, something he had been searching for the last few years."

XVIII

Atrin left the Rainbow Conclave just after the foundation stone laying ceremony. He asked his driver to drop him at the docking station near Tarulia village. "Sir, it will take a longer time, maybe more than three hours. Actually, people from nearby villages have filled the roads today, so there is a bit of a jam. Everyone wants to see the stars at the Conclave. And how can we blame them? There has never been such a big function in this area."

The driver was oblivious to the fact that Atrin had put on his AirPods. He continued blabbering about the mega event. He too, seemed to be in a happy mood as it had given him an opportunity to meet his parents at Tarulia village. He had requested them many times to stay with him at Nabinagar, but the wounds of the 2004 Panch Mukhi mishap had not yet healed. His parents still wished to live in Tarulia, waiting for their friends who never returned that fateful night.

Atrin was listening to the recording of Lenkesh's last conservation with him. Hearing Papa's voice made him emotional. It made him feel that Papa was somewhere near. It was due to Surti and Sanya at NODO that he had a copy of this recording, the last interaction between the father and son. The two never met again.

Surti and Sanya were his eyes and ears at NODO. They respected Papa a lot as he had helped them in getting married in court. Actually, Surti and Sanya's familial animosity had a long history. The two families had a land dispute, and the matter was in court. The situation got aggravated when Surti's grandfather hit Sanya's grandfather in a rage, and the blow proved to be fatal. The death of Sanya's grandfather closed all doors of negotiation on the land dispute.

A few months later, Surti's grandfather was shot dead by unknown assailants. Although the police could not trace the shooters, Surti's family was sure that the kill was ordered by Sanya's family. The two families had only one thing in common now. And it was revenge.

Hence, Surti and Sanya knew well that their parents would never agree to this marriage. It was then that they approached Lenkesh. He readily arranged their court marriage and became a witness, too. He had promised to speak to their parents on the upcoming Makar Sankranti (14th January, considered as New Year). "They will definitely listen to me," Lenkesh said. But he never lived to see the dawn of Makar Sankranti, as he was checkmated by Dr Chandrasi on the ill-fated night of December 2004.

The passage of time had only escalated Atrin's pain and sorrow. He had been preparing himself for this battle for quite some time now. He could have easily hired a person for this job, but it was deeply personal. He enrolled himself in a foreign university and got a degree in Oceanology. He interned at research institutes in Australia to gain hands-on experience. It was not easy for businessman Atrin to switch to Oceanology and step into Lenkesh's shoes. But a couple of years of rigorous training ensured his transformation into an expert and oceans became his core business.

Since the day Lenkesh disappeared, it was a battle for him and "When have battles been ethical?" Thought Atrin. With brimming eyes, he stammered, "Papa's name must be cleared. He gave his life to NODO, yet there was no official statement or record about that ill-fated night." Instead of acknowledging his great achievements and numerous accomplishments, they tarnished his reputation.

"My father was not a traitor. I will complete his dream project. I will snatch my father's rightful dues. I am going to carry forward Papa's visionary project at all costs."

As he looked out of the window, the lab cum docking station's silhouette was getting visible now.

"Go and spend time with your parents at Tarulia, and come back in the evening tomorrow around five," said Atrin as he alighted from the car at the main building. Soon, he was inside the highly secure precincts. The outer lights had already been switched off. All the scientists and technicians had been given special passes to attend the Rainbow Conclave.

Atrin wanted to be alone in the lab before executing this operation. His father's name had been denigrated, and who else but a son could reinstate his honour? He slipped into a sleeping pod and closed his eyes. The big day was just a few hours away. Tossing impatiently in the pod, he waited for dawn to mark the onset of sunrise.

"They questioned my Papa's ethics and, without giving him a fair trial, decimated his reputation! Just as Chandrasi ruined Papa's name, I am going to sink her Project TECHSIKA. With that, her name and rectitude will be destroyed forever.

The National Oceanic Defence Organisation will go down in history as a money guzzler of the taxpayers. NODO forgot Papa's contribution, and I will ensure that the nation consigns NODO to oblivion and the organisation is disgraced publicly."

He got up from the sleep pod and began pacing in the room. The wall had numerous photos of Lenkesh working at NODO, and he stopped at one particular photo, which had Chandrasi in the background. He looked at her with disdain.

And then a wicked smile swept his face. "You really think that the plane hijack and Ransomware attacks were foiled by you and NODO? You live in a fool's paradise, Chandrasi. The two hijackers were mere foot soldiers who didn't even know that they were on a suicide mission. They were not aware of the presence of MNG capsules in their bodies. It would have ensured their death, irrespective of the outcome of the hijack.

You backstabbed my Papa to get a promotion. Wasn't that all, hidden under the garb of ethics and morals?If I wished to kill you, that was easy. But I wanted you to live. I wanted to see the fear in your eyes. I wanted to show your haplessness to the world. Shouldn't everyone get a chance to see how weak and flippant Chandrasi is?"

It was still dark outside as the notification blinked on his mobile. It was a message from SS, 'AMBAK-the EYE has been activated.' That was a bit unusual. "Was it just a routine exercise, or had his plan been exposed?" Wondered Atrin.

"AMBAK-the EYE would easily detect my submersible; I can't take the risk." He knew it was designed to see anything and everything around TECHSIKA as its eagle eye roved in the deep ocean, picking up even slight disturbances.

But there was no question of backing out now. He rechecked the data and looked at the approximate location of TECHSIKA.

It had taken years of research and underwater expeditions for Atrin and his team to triangulate the new location. Had it not been for Surti and Sanya's valuable insider information, this discovery would have definitely taken a longer time. So, whatever Surti and Sanya at NODO could lay their hands on, they relayed the information to him.

"Ah, that seems to be the gift from Surti," said Atrin, looking at the packet on the centre table. Yesterday, he had sent a Good Luck GIF (their code for communicating that a parcel is on the way). As Atrin opened the packet, there was a diver suit and a tag: "Launched today - special suit for NODO divers, to be used when AMBAK-the EYE is active". It was dated the fourteenth of March.

"Oh, Surti! I don't know how to thank you. You have resolved the situation so easily. This suit ensures that our plan is on track. Papa would have been proud of you today," he said, clutching at the suit.

He had never met SS in person before Lenkesh's death. It was Viraj who introduced him to SS as Lenkesh's main collaborator and financier in ocean explorations. Atrin was so impressed by the ruthlessness with which he dealt with the enemies.

A couple of years ago, Sitara Devi's government had won a protracted legal battle and had taken over SS's assets.

Compensation had been offered to him, but how could he agree to that? It was way below his standards. "A king could never accept alms"; he shouted at the government emissary and left his majestic palace forever.He left everything behind and never came back.

But was forgetting or forgiving in his blood? "No,he was just waiting for an opportunity to strike. And when the time came, he hit with full force and ensured that it was a knockout blow. She had forcibly taken away his palace, and he snatched her name and reputation. With the curtains coming down on the political career of Sitara Devi, the scores were level."

His mining business was already raking in the mullah, and Durjan was proving to be a good gatekeeper. He conveniently side-lined Durjan and now treated him like a groundsman. The line between legal and illegal businesses was blurred since the beginning of their association, but the word legit had now completely vanished from his dictionary as his business diversified rapidly.

SS was hurt by the way the system treated him. His ancestors had ruled these lands for ages, and hence his belief was, 'Once a ruler, Always a ruler'. These lands belonged to him. His writ should have run rather than a government servant's. And that is why he needed to set an example so that no one ever dared to question his authority. And what better than the drug scandal sounding the death knell for the sitting Chief Minister Sitara Devi and her son Victor?

Atrin wanted to redeem his father's honour, and humiliate Chandrasi, whereas SS was happy with the money–that the international cartels were offering him in lieu of TECHSIKA. Dr Chandrasi and NODO were the main obstructions in their path, and hence, they both joined hands to eliminate their common enemy.

The morning sun rays and chirping of birds reminded Atrin that it was time for action. He put on the specially designed underwater suit sent by Surti and moved towards the motor boat waiting for him. The turquoise water and orange sky appeared soothingly mystical.

The water's mightiness and magnificence increased as he moved away from the shore. Soon, the container ship was in sight, and Atrin climbed the accommodation ladder to get in. He went straight to the lab on board and checked the cameras himself for any unusual activity. The ocean looked calm and serene.

The container ship had been standing in the ocean for the last six days due to some mechanical problem. Every morning the technicians used to come in the motor boat. His plan of a stagnant container ship was already in place so that there was no change in the satellite imagery. Hence, Atrin knew that his arrival won't be noticed.

Ocean had been friendly every time Atrin went for a rendezvous. He was slowly dropped into the water, and the tether was disconnected after a few seconds. Now he was on his own. He slipped beneath the tranquil surface and plunged downward towards the coral reef.

He was expecting the orange and yellow tube sponges to be scattered across the reef just as it was in his previous dive.But the ocean looked slightly different as Atrin experienced slight discomfort in his chest.

"Was it due to nitrogen narcosis (rupture of the deep) or depression sickness (DCS, commonly known as bends)?" He was feeling a bit giddy as if some weight was pulling him down. He tried to move closer towards the mineral reserves, but the crackling and snapping sounds made by the crustaceans and fishes seemed to be vibrating his body.

Atrin could see himself underwater in a remote reef with various forms of biodiversity. He looked at his stopwatch, "how come he was moving faster than the original plan?" His heart throbbed rapidly as he felt being drowned into some kind of black hole.

"Oh My God, why did I not see through her plan? It was a set-up and I walked right into the middle of it. I have been trapped by Chandrasi. If the diving suit's not working, that means the cover of Surti and Sanya has been blown. They are now sitting ducks." Atrin said as he tried in vain to pull himself away from the magnetic force.

As he was drowning, Atrin could see a red light. "Was he seeing the sun? He struggled to move towards the light but in vain." All the wealth and properties of PENAK Associates could not save its owner. Today his wish list had just one item, he wanted to go home.

Ocean gave him so much; rather it has bestowed generous blessings on the entire humanity. The ocean's contribution in climate moderation as the largest natural reservoir of carbon is humongous to be easily forgotten. Yet it is human greed which neglects the contribution and causes imbalance in the ecosystem.

"Acknowledging the ocean as a living being, just as our ancestors did is the need of the hour." Realisation dawned upon Atrin but it was too late.

Dr Chandrasi had leaked the information about the activation of AMBAK-the EYE on purpose. She wanted to avoid any skirmishes on the Press Conference day, so she used its invincibility to scare her opponents. She knew that nobody would dare to take a chance against AMBAK-the EYE.

Then she spread the story about a special diver suit, and Surti fell for it.Perhaps his promotion gave some sort of overconfidence and he did not cross check the origin of the suit. These underwater suits were actually meant to drag the user down due to the ferromagnetic properties in its soles.

"This way, she killed two birds with one stone. Surti and Sanya were exposed, and Atrin's identity came out in the open. The masks of Surti, Sanya and Atrin were blown in a single move. She beat Atrin at his own game."

Going down, Atrin recalled the stories of Sagar Matha, the sea angel who is believed to be the guardian of the treasures of the Ocean. He has been there for ages as the protector of marine biodiversity.

Sagar Matha, meaning the forhead of Ocean in local Kharki language is deeply revered by the people. He is the one who fills the ocean with abundant and diverse life. From tiny zooplanktons to large whales, it nurtures them all with care. But if its tranquility is disturbed, it gets angry.

'Whatever is thrown into the ocean, Sagar Matha throws it back with double vengeance.'

The final hour had arrived, the fifteenth of March, six a.m. The drones had sent photographs of a palatial green building in deep forest. From a distance, it looked like a dense bunch of trees hugging each other affectionately.

With the advance party moving ahead, the NIU Chief and Kraman reached the state highway on dotted time. There was a small opening on the left-hand side, enough for three or four men to walk. The vehicle could not go farther, so they decided to go on foot.

"The forest is so dense, Sir; I hope we are on the right track."

"Don't worry, Kraman, I can see my men over there."

As the clearing got a bit larger, they could see sun rays falling on the vine-covered walls of the colossal green building named Shark Kothi with the ancient symbol of Ouroboros engraved on its top. "Ah, it is the same building Viraj was referring to. It seems we are closer to our target," said De Silva Sir as he instructed his men to surround the place and cover all the exit routes.

The NIU Chief rang the doorbell. An old man in late seventies opened the door and spoke in a drowsy tone, "Sahib is not at home. He has gone for the morning walk. He would be back in an hour. By the way, he did not tell me about any guests coming today. So, I can't let you in till Sahib comes back."

"I know that," the NIU Chief said with a broad smile while shaking hands with the old man. "We are childhood friends and went to the same school. He was in a senior class, but we were mates in the horse riding sessions. I wanted my visit to be a surprise, that is why I did not inform him earlier. I have returned to Niskashi after a long time. The place has changed a lot. Even his palace is now a government guesthouse. How is his family? Where are they?"

The expression on the old man's face changed from suspicion to melancholy. "Ah, everything has changed here. The chote Kunwar[42] and Sahib are not on talking terms. He never comes to meet Sahib. Other than his business associates, Sahib has very few visitors."

Both NIU Chief and Kraman were waiting for the soluble pad of sedatives (which was pressed onto the old man's palm while shaking his hand) to take effect. "You are looking a bit drowsy; let me help you," said Kraman assisting him to a sofa in the lounge, and soon, the old man fell asleep.

"Nice story, Chief," said an amused Dr Chandrasi, looking at the live streaming of Shark Kothi. "For a moment, I really believed all that you said. But, where has Kraman disappeared?" Her voice command activated the side screen to start streaming the visuals of Kraman. "Ah, there he is, gazing intently at the painting in the drawing room." The cameras zoomed to the full-size painting of the Gold of Kinabalu adorning the walls. "Is this the same painting SP had bragged about? Is this the same house where the housewarming party was held? And above all, is this the mysterious man's house?"

"Kraman, come here fast," it was Chief De Silva's high-pitched voice. He was staring at the huge snake tank, almost

---

[42] *young scion*

the size of a big hall. There were large poisonous snakes kept in separate enclosures, all lying still. "Are they sedated?" Asked Kraman. "I have never seen so many snakes in one house. It is so weird"

Only one enclosure was empty. The board on it read, 'Saw-Scaled Viper' and 'Blue Malaysian Coral snake'. Although none of the snakes moved, their sight was so terrifying that they quickly closed the door behind them.

"I think there is someone in the room. I heard a voice," said Kraman as they crossed to the next room. Both stood still and tried to listen. A very feeble sound, 'Help Me,' was coming from the room. As they peeped through the window, Kraman shouted. "I can see Shlok, my colleague." Both of them entered the room and opened the ropes with which his legs had been tied. "Helicopter ambulance will be here in ten minutes; your friend will be fine," said De Silva Sir. "Get him some water. He looks completely dehydrated."

"I had information from my sources that a clandestine meeting was being held at a house in Harekrishna Nagar, so I decided to do a sting operation," said Shlok in a halting tone. "But the guards saw me. They kicked and punched me mercilessly. When I regained consciousness, I was here in this room, all tied up in ropes. Initially, they had tied my hands and mouth also. But as I became weaker, they removed the tape from my mouth and freed my hands, thinking that I was anyway, going to die."

Kraman helped him in drinking water and said, "Take rest, Shlok. You are very weak; let the doctor examine you first."I called your family and told them you are safe.But I think it would be better if you spoke to them, they were pretty worried after your disappearance.

“Actually I had a map of this place, but lost it somewhere” said Shlok in a halting tone. “Don’t worry, it is safe. But what do you know about TECHSIKA ?” Asked Kraman.

“Well, I heard that for the first time at Harekrishna Nagar . It was an auction for TECHSIKA with many foreigners ready to pay millions of dollars for it.There was a mad rush amongst the buyers as they continued bidding higher amounts.I was trying to set my camera, when the guards hit me and I fell down.”

“The Helicopter ambulance has arrived, let me help you and don’t stress yourself too much. Get well soon,”said Kraman hugging him tightly.

The team was checking all the rooms, but the owner was not at home; perhaps the housekeeper was right. Kraman was looking at the paintings when his hand accidentally touched its mid area. It appeared hollow. There was a slight vibrating sound as Kraman tapped the painting again.

“It’s strange,”he said tapping it forcefully this time. The wall swirled a bit, just enough to access the incoming fax. It was addressed to Maharaja Shakti Shubhankar, requesting him to stop using his email id ss@xyz.com as attempts were being made by investigative authorities to trace its owner.

Kraman sank into the chair beside him. “It is unbelievable!” Said Dr Chandrasi as he flashed the paper to the screens. The NIU Chief called his backup team to secure the area immediately.

Maharaja Shakti Shubhankar was doing his usual Surya Namaskar as he saw the Saw-Scaled Viper and the Blue Malaysian Coral snake moving towards him. "Oh, my babies, you did such a marvellous job at Kavya's house. She was meddling too much in our affairs. I tried a truce by inducting her as a majority stakeholder in PENAK Associates, but she still wanted to make the matter public. I asked her to join us, but she made it an 'us versus her' battle! I tried my best to explain to her that we had invested massively in the ocean exploration project. Hence, we should be the ones having the first right over it. But she was not willing to budge from her high moral ground."

She had the audacity to send me the mail, threatening to expose me. But you two ensured that it was her last mail. I may have lost my estates, but I still own the people; no one can dare to refuse my orders.

I helped so many people, including Lenkesh. It was his last email requesting me to continue his research work that touched my heart. For the last few years, I have been helping Atrin's research, which is soon going to change the way we look at our oceans. My foreign collaborators are eagerly waiting to buy TECHSIKA. For them, price is no consideration; they just want a confirmation from me.

Atrin has great respect for his father, unlike my son, who denies even my existence. Yet, see my large-heartedness! I got Kamtej out of the guest house, where he was imprisoned due to his protest march at Sona Ghaati. I just had to make a phone call, and he was free!

That journalist, Shlok tried to click my pictures with the foreign collaborators at Harekrishna Nagar. He interrupted my party, yet I was kind enough to not throw him inside the snake house. He is now resting next to it, "stung by the sting operation".

It was once again SP, who alerted me about Shlok. He is my true friend and we intertwine like a covalent bond.

"Are you missing Durjan? He looked at the snakes with a roguish smile. You won't see him anymore. Yesterday, my sharpshooter closed his story forever at the Rainbow Conclave. He paid the price for stabbing my back. I created Viraj's identity, protecting Durjan in the process, and hence had a right to erase him."

Now, with his death, police will reach a dead end and will be forced to close all investigations. The evidence is stacked against him as per the financial records and money trails. "All my businesses are in Viraj's name, and it is his identity documents, photographs and signatures everywhere. The police will find nothing against me, not a single shred of evidence. They won't be able to trace even a single penny to me," Maharaja said confidently.

"Come, my babies, as a gesture gift, I am not going to sedate you for a week." He held them close, moving his palms gently over their shining, slithery bodies. They had been his companions for years at Shark Kothi. He felt their grip was becoming stiffer, or were they reciprocating his appreciation? Maharaja wondered as he closed his eyes, oblivious to the fact that their hooked tongues were pointing towards him. Then there was the powerful hiss sound, swift as lightning, and soon, Maharaja's lifeless body slumped to the ground.

The NIU team was checking for fingerprints before marking the exhibit code on the evidences when they saw Kraman staring at the empty gift box and Gold of Kinabalu orchids."How could Shakti Shubhankar be so heartless to send the gift of death, the harbinger of doom to Kavya ? And as if it was not enough, he is keeping them like a decorative trophy in the Shark Kothi. I can't stand it." He said moving towards the garden.

The sniffer dog squad and their handlers had been pressed in action in the area around Shark Kothi.Soon reinforcement arrived in the forest and sleuths were all over the place.

"Why did Maharaja Shakti Shubhankar have such an affinity towards the Gold of Kinabalu orchids?" Asked Dr Chandrasi. "There are just a few wild flowers in his garden but no orchids! We have checked his passport; he has never been to Malaysia. Rather, he fears flying as per his medical history! Then why is he fascinated by this particular painting?"

"That baffles me too," said De Silva Sir. "He neither looks like an art connoisseur nor an anthophile (a lover of flowers). We found no other paintings or artistic decorative pieces in this Kothi." My team has just now spoken to the administrator of his palace at Niskashi, and he told that when the palace was converted to a government guesthouse, the Maharaja refused to take any of his belongings with him other than this painting of Gold of Kinabalu orchids.

"The presence of this painting is mysterious. I will ask the forensic team to take the painting to their lab and get the results on priority. Because if he was not hiding something, why did he choose this Shark Kothi in such a dense forest?"

"Where is Mugdha?" asked SP impatiently.

"Sir, she left early today and was looking very upset. Yesterday evening, there was a courier for her. Mamak ji's daughter, Mayuri Madam, waited in the lobby to personally deliver the packet. I told her to give the packet to me, but she declined," said Ramu Kaka.

SP was going through the morning newspaper but could not stop smiling at the last comment. Ramu Kaka has been with them since Mugdha was just five years old. The two gelled together very well, and soon Ramu was aware of all her likes and dislikes. SP was sometimes jealous that Ramu knew more than him about Mugdha's friends, gym schedules and even her Zumba dance trainer! "But why had Mayuri personally come to deliver the packet to Mugdha? She could have easily sent it through someone."

The mobile ringtone broke his chain of thoughts. It was his secretary confirming that Lawyer Narain Mishra had reached the court. "Sir, he has a hundred per cent success record in bail cases, and is going to remain unbeaten today also. I have seen Mugdha Madam's car in the parking lot. It seems she arrived early."

SP finished his breakfast at leisure and proceeded to the court just like a normal working day. The morning papers were full of yesterday's Rainbow Conclave pictures, with SP's photo being splashed on the cover page itself (courtesy: Babil).

The clock struck ten as the Hon'ble Judge entered the courtroom, and everyone rose in his honour. Mugdha had rushed in a few seconds earlier. SP waved at her, but she seemed immersed in the files. Narain Mishra introduced himself as the lawyer of the defendant.

"And who is representing the state?"

"Your Honour, it is Mugdha Pradosh - Special Public Prosecutor."

There was stunned silence in the courtroom. Her words sounded like a gavel being hit on the table. Every head turned towards Mugdha. SP, who was standing along with his counsel, Narain Mishra, sank into the chair. He was feeling dizzy as the world around him came crashing down in a matter of seconds.

He seemed to be talking to himself: "She means the world to me. My whole life revolves around Mugdha, the apple of my eye. How can she go against me? No, there seems to be some mistake. Mugdha, please talk to me." He looked imploringly into her eyes.

But she chose to look the other way and began her deliberations in the courtroom – "We oppose the defendant's bail application as he is too dangerous for society and should not be allowed to roam free. We seek his case to be fast-tracked."

As Narain Mishra rose to speak, SP tugged at his arm and signalled him to keep silent. The Hon'ble Judge asked again, "Does the defendant have to say anything?" "No, my Lordship," Sr. Advocate Narain Mishra replied.

Today, in a matter of a few minutes, he lost everything. The ghosts from the past had returned to haunt him.Years ago,he snatched Kali Industries, the soul of Kali Babu and used it as the foundation to build his empire. 'But can buildings erected on the foundation of dead bodies last long?'

The mighty SP was today a loner; his universe had crumbled. He felt as if his heart had turned into a black hole with no room for light. What remained was just the empty space like a vacuum ! Today, he could perceive the anguish of Kadambari when she was deserted. He could feel the agony of Kavya when she was publicly disowned. SP betrayed the trust of people who counted on him. He did not accept Kavya as her daughter, and today, Mugdha denied his existence as a father. Karma hits back!!!

SP was ordered to be taken into custody by the Hon'ble Judge. Without Mugdha, life meant nothing for SP. He wished to seek forgiveness from Kadambari and Kavya, but it was too late. Destiny had delivered justice, and SP was at the receiving end today. Mayuri's eyes were brimming with tears as she sat in the courtroom holding her best friend Kavya's photograph close to her heart.

Meanwhile the NIU had registered the case against SP under non bailable sections of Money Laundering Act.

Mugdha was still holding the diary of Kavya in her hands. Not once did she look at SP when he was being taken away by the police. She had not slept the whole night after reading the diary. A young and budding life was cut short in such a brutal way, but what was Kavya's fault?

As Mugdha stepped out of the Courtroom, she asked Mayuri about the list of charities that Kavya was supporting. " I can not replace your best friend , but will try to continue her good work. I want to work for those charities and spread cheer and sunshine, just as she did." Mayuri hugged her and smiled, " Let's begin from Sona Ghaati ."

People were glued to the webcast as live proceedings of Kamtej's plea in the Supreme Court began. The court came down heavily on the Jan Sampark Party's government for showing undue favour to PENAK Associates, as the entire exercise seemed to be vitiated by favouritism. The court observed that the Sona Ghaati land takeover was not only in violation of the land acquisition laws but also in breach of environmental laws, as any construction on that land could cause irreversible damage to the ecosystem.

"What is the hurry to complete this project without environmental clearances ? Even the bidding processes seem to be flouting the National Vigilance Commission's guidelines. Do you think, we are a banana Republic ?" The Hon'ble Judges minced no words in expressing their anguish.

The Hon'ble Court further noted that a river flowed through the acquired land, and giving control of it to PENAK Associates was a disregard of the law. The court was critical of the government for showering undue largesse at the cost of farmers' interests.

The Hon'ble Bench repeatedly observed that the government should hold its hands until the matter is heard at length, prompting the Additional Solicitor General to give an undertaking to the Hon'ble Court that farmers will not be displaced from Sona Ghaati and status quo will be maintained.

"The residents of Sona Ghaati must be elated today," thought Kraman as he recalled his cab driver's words, "When no one owns nature, how can someone sell it?"

The live telecast of Dr Chandrasi's press conference began at 5 p.m.

"It is my honour today to present TECHSIKA – TECH for Sustainable(S) & Inclusive(I) Kinētikos(K) Amritkalam(A), the foundry capable of manufacturing nanometer chips. It is going to be our Swarna kaal [43], when we will no longer be dependent on other nations for our requirement of chips. Our indigenous project has been blessed with mysterious reserves, which are a perfect core material for our homegrown technology." she said proudly. The screens began relaying live footage of the ocean bed where huge mounds of mineral reserve was shining.

"Nature has blessed us with bounties, yet we show utter carelessness and disregard for her," Dr Chandrasi said. "We need to realise that our bond with nature is so sacrosanct that any attempt to break this relationship can cause havoc for our future generations. Our coasts should be emblematic of health, vitality and vigour rather than being the mining mafia's den.

TECHSIKA is based on our synergy with nature. As you can see on the screens, the reserves contain precious and mysterious minerals. We have developed technology to enable the electrons in it to move freely and quickly without much scattering, making it an ideal chip material for electronic devices. Right there on the screen, is our indigineous Extreme Ultra Violet lithography machine to pack more transistors into a single chip.This will enable us to go for mass production of chips at affordable rates.

---

[43] *golden era*

Chips, as we know are at the heart of all modern computing devices. They bring power to tools as simple as a light switch and as complex as a fighter jet. Be it electronics, automobiles, data centres, computers, phones, critical infrastructure, military systems, you name it, and the chips form the backbone," said Dr Chandrasi.

Our tests have confirmed that as a semiconductor[44], with superior electrical conductivity, along with high charge carrier mobility and large active surface area, it is bound to be a game changer in the semiconductor industry. The race in this industry is about getting smaller, faster and cheaper chips, and we will soon be there at the top.

One of the reporters raised her hand, "How did you find these reserves?"

"Well, it is the result of years of hard work of my team at NODO," said Dr Chandrasi. "As we all know that Samudra Manthan leads to ratnas[45]. This is a gift of Samudra Manthan for us and our future generations."

"Is it true that Maharaja Shakti Shubhankar's dead body was found about nine hundred metres away from Shark Kothi?"

It was Babil's voice from the 'Janta ka Sewak' channel.You mean, the father of eminent lawyer Kamtej? There were murmurs in hall. "Since he left his palace at Niskashi,we never heard about him. Where was he, all these years?"Asked a reporter.

---

[44] *Semiconductors are a class of crystalline solids intermediate in electrical conductivity between insulators and conductors*

[45] *jewels*

“I think the question is for me,” said NIU Chief De Silva. Adjusting his mike, he looked straight into the eyes of Babil. “I wish our friend could tell us more about Maharaja Shakti Shubhankar and his Shark Kothi”. Babil was in trouble, as he saw a plainclothes policeman approaching him. He wiped the sweat off his face and exited the hall in a hurry.

“Some of you might be wondering why I am here today. Well, we had reports of a virus outbreak in this area. Initially the symptoms were mild, but the mutated strain proved highly infectious.Whether Maharaja Shakti Shubhankar’s death is related to this virus attack, we will have to wait for the test results,” he said and asked Dr Chandrasi to continue.

“We join the nation today in celebrating TECHSIKA. National Oceanic Defence Organisation dedicates it to our Motherland,”said Dr Chandrasi amidst cheers and claps of appreciation from her team and the media.”

As she moved out of the hall, the first thing that she did was to call the lab director. “Yes Ma’am, the medicines would be available to the villagers of Sona Ghaati within a week. I know they have suffered a lot, but soon everything is going to be okay.There is another good news for them, Kamtej is setting up a hospital at Sona Ghaati, Zaidi Healthcare.” Her face beamed with happiness and joy, as she entered her room.

It had been a gruelling yet fulfilling day as she looked at her father’s portrait with gratitude. As a child, she often asked him to buy her wings so that she could fly like a bird. And he would say, “You cannot buy wings. You have to earn them, just like these birds.” She dialled her Appa, “I got my wings today……”

Politics has an essence of unpredictability! The exit polls for the three states were wrong this time. Mamak's Jan Sampark Party received a drubbing at the hands of the electorate. The verdict was loud and clear.

The vote was in favour of the policies and ideals that Mamak Vragji and his Jan Sampark Party once stood for. In the electoral battle between 'Power to People' and 'Governance by Middlemen' ,the voter had chosen the former and rejected the latter. Democracy is about people and their choices and the people had exercised their franchise and voted against Jan Sampark Party.

Perhaps his proximity to people like Shyam Pradosh didn't go down well with the electorate. The election results were a wake-up call for Mamak that he had to reinvent himself to stay relevant.

"Was there any ambiguity in the writing on the wall? Only for those who choose to close their eyes."

The lab results came late at night on the fifteenth of March. As the Gold of Kinabalu orchid painting was being scanned through the advanced Blue-Green-Digital device, certain unusual patterns cropped up. "Maybe it is due to the natural colours of the painting. That is why these patterns look bizarre," thought the lab technician and checked again.

But there were many double helixes, twisted like human DNA[46] throughout the painting. Rather, they seemed to be drawn on the original painting at a later date. He immediately

---

[46] *Deoxyribonucleic acid*

called his seniors. The pattern looked intriguing, and the NIU team decided to use the special dye that lightens the colours of the paintings in the same sequence in which they are applied. The original colours on the painting began to fade fast once the dye was applied to it. The double helixes were getting clearer .

"OMG! At the centre of the strands, encrypted messages are embedded.I can also see numbers randomly written on the helixes"shouted the technician. It took some time for the NIU team to decode that data. There was a plethora of information - names, phone numbers, bank account numbers and everything that Shakti Shubhankar had ever dealt with, since he left his palace at Niskashi. One of the biggest search and seizure operation in NIU history was soon underway!

The next morning, Kraman was in flight again. He opened his backpack and took out Suchita didi's envelope with a big smile. Both times, in his to and fro journey to Nabinagar, the specially designed, handmade envelope had been his companion. But this time, it had her address. "The festival of Rakshabandhan has arrived early for me and didi. How will I repay this debt of NIU Chief De Silva Sir?"

The death of Maharaja Shakti Shubhankar saddened Lakhna. But his grief did not last long. He soon received a phone call. The order was for three pairs of deadly snakes.. The cocktail of greed and corruption had found a companion – Shenoy Seth (SS).

It is a big world…….